"Gratitude Attitude promotes Spiritual Generosity"

I am eternally grateful to the following people who have encouraged my dream at being a fiction writer.

All my family who always support me in all I do.

Kim, my loving eldest daughter, who has a busy life of her own but put up with hearing about the book, editing the book and preparing it for publishing. She always does everything to help 'mom' manifest her dreams.

My friend Dale Haggerty, my spiritual sister, who read ... reread ... reread 'til her eyes nearly burned out of her head editing and critiquing checking to see facts matched up and when I got hung up encouraged me into finishing it. And who after all the reading loved the book especially the ending.

My granddaughter Mya, who read it and said, "It's good Grandma."

THANK YOU

Forward

A child is missing from his home and RCMP Sergeant Sean Fitzgerald arrives to find a crowd gathered outside the home. Among the curiosity seekers and news reporters is an attractive young woman trying to get his attention ... but he has a job to do ... she will have to wait.

Back at the detachment Sean rides an emotional rollercoaster as he meets the young woman up close and personal in the reception room. He discovers she is a well known psychic, credited with helping to solve a number of other cases in the lower mainland area of British Columbia, Canada.

Joanna Lenardi's hypnotic, velvet brown eyes unnerve Sean as she turns to greet him As she speaks, Sean experiences mixed feelings of tranquility and excitement which is totally foreign to him.

Sean's down-to-earth, practical, scientific based method of police work comes face to face with the need to take all the help he can get. Even though his personal opinions that psychic work is all done with 'a smoke and mirror technique,' Sean knows he cannot ignore any possible lead no matter how slim the chance of it being valid.

Further complications arise when Sean finds he has a great physical attraction for this young woman and also finds he has to admit she exhibits abilities to know things both about him and the case that she seems to be getting from some other source outside of the world he lives in ...

Missing

Chapter 1

The shrill sound of the phone, on the night stand, pierced through Sean's deep sleep. Almost knocking the phone to the floor, he managed to flip the receiver the right side up and mumbled into the phone, "Sergeant Fitzgerald."

The urgent voice of his partner, Sergeant Leanne Chapman on the other end of the phone answered, "Sorry to wake you Sean. We have a missing boy in the Newton area. The Amber Alert is sent out already. We need you to meet us here as soon as possible."

"Text me the details Leanne." Sean replied as he placed his feet on the cool hardwood floor and headed for his bathroom. "I'm on my way."

Pulling up in front of the three bedroom basement home, in an older residential area of Surrey, Sean noted the media and other curious onlookers from the neighbourhood had already gathered at the scene. It was obvious the neighbours were all out there as well. You could feel an anxiety building throughout the crowd.

"Sergeant Fitzgerald!" one of the TV reporters called out, "Can you tell us what you know so far about this young boy's disappearance?"

"When we know something, you will be the first to hear about it. But for now, let us do our jobs. Okay guys?" Sean said in a friendly, reassuring tone.

Most of the media people had a long relationship with Sean. They respected him for his forthright attitude and also knew he understood they too had a job to do. If they were respectful and ethical in their association, he would indeed keep them up to date with the information he could share with them.

Continuing to walk towards the house, Sean noticed one woman in particular, from the back of the crowd, trying to get his attention he was unable to discern what she was saying, then as he reached the front door he heard, "Sergeant Fitzgerald, I would like to help you find the boy if you will let me."

Turning towards the direction of the voice, Sean saw a very attractive, slim built, thirty-something, woman making her way to the front of the crowd.

Sean found himself looking into the most hypnotic, velvet brown eyes he had ever seen. For a moment Sean felt he had lost all contact with his present reality and had travelled into another time or place.

At that moment Leanne opened the door and Sean stepped in. "Have you talked to that woman out there Leanne?" He asked, while still reeling from the affect of this encounter he just experienced. To himself he wondered, "Am I losing my mind? What in Hell just happened out there?" He consciously forced himself to listen to Leanne as she answered his question.

"Not yet Sean. She is a local psychic who is said to have been a great deal of help, in similar missing people cases, in our area. A few people in our own detachment sing her praises and claim she is authentic. They have worked with her and swear she has amazing abilities to know things and see things that are not of the reasonable, rational world we work in. Leanne then added "Myself, well the jury is still out on whether psychics are of any use in an investigation."

"Well the jury isn't out in my case" Sean scoffs. "Magic tricks, 'smoke and mirrors' coupled with a lot of lucky guess work, that is what I think of so-called psychic abilities. Right now we need some good old fashion police work mixed with modern technology if we want to find out what is going on here. So tell me, what do we have so far?"

As Leanne filling Sean in on the details explaining the mother claims the boy, Tommy Byers, went missing off the front steps of the house somewhere between 6 a.m. when mom gave a bottle to his baby sister and 9 a.m. when she and her live-in boyfriend got up to find him no longer in his bed. They say young Tommy had obviously wet his bed through the night, got up, changed out of the wet pyjamas into his blue shorts, and blue and white striped T-shirt he was wearing the day before and that is all they know. A neighbour, who arrives home from work around 6 each morning, says it is not unusual to see the boy sitting outside on the porch steps early in the morning but he could not recall for sure if he was there this morning when he came home."

"The first officers on the scene have interviewed the mother and the live-in boyfriend. Their stories seem to be very much the same" Leanne stated, "and the forensic team has gone to work getting all of their evidence in and around the home. The K-9 handlers have been over the inside and outside of the house with no definite trail to show if the boy left the property or where he might have gone."

While Leanne was talking, Sean was observing the deplorable condition of the home. It was quite obviously there was a party here the night before. The overwhelming mixture of odours from cigarette butts pilled high in the ashtrays, empty liquor bottles, partly filled beer bottles, glasses, and fast food containers strewn all over the living room, assaulted Sean's senses making him feel nauseated.

Thoughts and feelings of his own childhood rushed back into his consciousness. "Poor kid," Sean said to himself. "Five years old ... no one to look after him." It was hard to tell if he was referring to Tommy or himself at that age. One thing for sure, Sean had to detach from the emotional parallel between himself and this young, missing child or he would be of no help to the boy or himself as the lead investigator on the case.

Leanne's voice brought him back to the now time as they entered the kitchen. As Sean moved through to the kitchen he again had a momentary flash back to his own childhood. He loved his mom with all his heart, but no matter how hard he tried he could not change the path of destruction she chose to travel. Sean brought himself back with a silent reprimand to himself "Let it go Sean ... you cannot change the past ..." echoed in his head.

Sean observed the kitchen that was even worse than the living room. There was not one flat surface of the kitchen that was not piled high with books, food, papers, dishes, empty cans and bottles. The waste basket was full to the brim, garbage falling out of overflowing bags sitting on the floor. The laundry area, off the kitchen, was a mixture of dirty clothes on the floor and on top of the machines and clean clothes hanging out of the open dryer door. Nodding to Constable Suzy Wong, to acknowledge her, Sean moved towards the mother. Leanne said "Ms Byers ... this is Sergeant Sean Fitzgerald. Sergeant Fitzgerald this is Tommy Byers, our missing boy's mother, Ms Byers."

"Just call me Marilyn," she said as she offered her hand to Sean." Marilyn Byers was a far cry from what one would expect of a grieving mother. Her thick dyed black hair was in a French braid that hung down the centre of her back. She had taken great care in doing her make-up and choosing her clothes. A low cut t-shirt which showed off her well developed bosom, and form fitting shorts with her high heeled sandals exposed shapely legs. This impeccable attire seemed very out of place considering the state of the home she lived in. Her whole meticulous appearance and her demeanor also seemed very strange for a mother whose son was missing.

Sean had long ago learned not to judge the situation by the behaviour of the people involved as grief will react on each person in a different way. He also knew jumping too quickly to a conclusion, without facts to back up the accusation, often lead many a good investigator 'down the prime rose path' and often jaded the investigator's objectivity.

Taking her hand in a tender motion he patted the top of it in a reassuring manner saying, "We need to get all the information we can to help find your little boy. Constable Wong will continue to take down everything you can remember and I will be back to talk to you in a little while. Anything ... no mattèr how insignificant as it may seem ...

will help us. So, help Constable Wong as much as you can." Then Sean left with Leanne to go into the master bedroom where the common law husband was being questioned by the newest member of the team, Constable Brandon Ellis.

Both Brandon and Suzy are uniformed officers on special assignment to the missing children team and are very valuable team members, as they, and Leanne had specialized training at the academy in interrogation methods for missing or abducted children. Sean had been given training in profiling in addition to the same training the rest of the team had, so there was no doubt that the best the RCMP had to offer were in this home. This would give Tommy Byers the best chance of being brought home safely.

It was important to get together to hear what each member of the team had learned. Everyone knew the best chance of finding the boy is in the first forty-eight hours, so this afternoon, when they all returned to their detachment, they would all share their information and observations with one another. This allows four set of eyes to examine the evidence and four people's individual awareness to discern the information both individually and as a team.

Sean had long time ago learned the value of team work and was grateful for the individual abilities that each member brought to the team. He may be lead investigator but that meant he brought the team together to share their abilities and knowledge. It would be team work that would bring Tommy home.

Chapter 2

The scene in the bedroom was as different as night and day from the one in the kitchen. Obviously younger by eight or ten years than Marilyn and in total contrast to Marilyn, the live–in boyfriend was exactly what you would expect of a man the morning after a 'party-hardy' evening. His beard unshaved, hair tussled and he seemed as if he just jumped into his work clothes from yesterday or maybe he had slept in them. Every pore of his body oozing with the sickening smell of alcohol, cigarettes and garlic food consumed last night. Sean noticed the young man frequently ran his hands through his hair in a motion that reflected a person in great distress. It was hard to tell if the young man's red eyes were a result of tears over Tommy's disappearance or a hangover from last night's wild party. Over and over again he lamented, "Oh my God ... where can he be ... where in Hell can he be?"

Leanne called him by name. "Don ..."   He brought up his head and met Sean's clear blue eyes with the look of a frightened animal.

"Sergeant Fitzgerald, this is Donald Aftonson, father of the baby Jana. He is Tommy's Stepdad." Then looking back to the young man asked, "Don, do you think you can tell Sergeant Fitzgerald what you recall of the events since putting the children to bed last night?" Then added, "Including exactly how and when you discovered Tommy missing?"

"I will do my best and thank you for being so patient with me," Don said to Leanne.

"Okay Don. You understand that I am recording this interview as well as taking notes." Sean stated. "You also realize you have a right to have a lawyer present and this is to be used in evidence in this case. You may wait to have a lawyer present as this evidence can and may be used against you in a court of law?"

Don nodded, and said, "Yes ... I do understand. I just want to find Tommy. I love him like he's my own kid."

"Thank you Don. Let's start with last night, what went on here? I'll need names of all the people who were here. Time frames of when the children were put to bed and when you last saw Tommy and many other facts? So let's start with last night. It appears you guys had quite the party. When did it start?"

"Actually, I wasn't here when the party started." Don said. "I was out trail riding on my bike with my buddies. When I got home around ten thirty last night the party was in full swing. The kids were still up running all over the place. Marilyn and her friends were well on their way to being wasted. Frankly, I was sore that the kids were not in bed so I told Marilyn to get her lazy ass in gear and get them into bed."

"Marilyn told me to get stuffed and if I didn't like it put them in bed myself. I got a bottle for Jana, changed her and put her in her PJ's and when I went to tuck Tommy into bed. He told me he hadn't had any supper."

"I told him to put on his PJ's while I made him a peanut butter and jam sandwich. I gave him a glass of milk and the sandwich and tucked him into bed. I told him to stay in bed. I said to him, 'You know Tommy; mommy will get angry if you upset her' and he hugged me and said. "I love you daddy Don."

"Those are the last words he said to me." Don choked back his emotions. "I hear them over and over in my head," choking back his emotions once more. It was apparent that he loves the boy.

At this point Sean asked what did Don know of the events of the morning and if he heard anything that would be unusual from the boy's room.

"Maybe we would not be looking for him now if I hadn't got wasted. I might have heard something." Don said, "Please Sergeant, find him and bring him home. I will promise you I'll look after him from now on." At that he buried his face back in his hands and his body shook with emotional sobs.

Sean waited for the sobbing to subside and asked him about this morning when he first got up and the events from there.

"I wish I had got up to Jana this morning." Don answered. He had not heard anything after he passed out at the party until Jana's crying woke him. He had ignored Jana's crying, pretending to be asleep. He knew that Marilyn would want to shut the baby up so she would get up and get a bottle for her. Don added that it was a habit of Jana to wake around 6 a.m. and Marilyn would stagger out of bed, fill a bottle and give it to Jana in her crib.

"Jana is a great baby. She would usually have her bottle and then go back to sleep or play quietly for the next few hours." Don said, and then added, "The next time I heard her fuss must have been around 9 a.m. and we both got up. "

"Then what happened?" Sean asked watching the pain come over Don's face again as he struggled to tell the rest of the story.

"Well ..." Don added, "Jana cried again around 9 a.m. and usually on the weekends I go to her on the second crying. I got up and brought Jana into our room. I changed her diaper and headed for the kitchen, then told Marilyn to get it in gear and go see to Tommy. As usual she went under loud protest to Tommy's room. Marilyn doesn't do mornings very well."

"Tommy wasn't in his room and I heard her yelling." "Where the hell are you Tommy? You've wet that friggin' bed again. I'm gonna kick your butt into the middle of next week when I get a hold of you."

"I heard her slamming doors. Janna started to cry so I picked her up and headed back up the hall to see what the yellin' was all about. I could hear Marilyn yelling outside then and when she came in she started to complain that she couldn't find him."

Marilyn yelled at me, "Check the neighbours, the little bugger is hiding somewhere. I'll call my sister Cheryl. He might have gone around to her house. She spoils him and he knows he is in deep shit over the bed wetting again."

"After we checked everyone we could think of" Don added "I convinced her we needed help and to call the police. That's all I can tell you. I wish I knew more." Don then went back to "Oh my God ... where can he be."

Being the lead investigator on the case Sean arranged with all of the officers involved with the investigation to meet with Leanne and him back at the detachment at 2 p.m. so they could all debrief each other on what evidence was available. They would need to talk to the family member's one at a time at the station and also find who were at this party last night. "Find out about the boy's natural father and check the family from both sides to get an insight into the child's life. He may have run off or there was still a possibility that one of the relatives may know where the boy is. Maybe took him out of this mess albeit without the permission of his the mother and thinking they were helping in some way."

One thing for sure ... Tommy needed to be found quickly.

Chapter 3

Sean dropped into the fresh food market in the mall behind the office and picked up some fruit and special lunch platter made up of potato salad, green salad, cold roasted chicken breast, pickles and a buttered dinner roll. He decided on his favourite beverage, chocolate milk-on-the-go and headed for the lunch room at the office.

He didn't realize until he started to eat that he had not eaten since 2 a.m. this morning. There had been a special awards dinner for his first partner who was retiring and Sean had been asked to be the M/C for the roast his family, friends and co-workers had planned as a surprise for him. It had been a great night as he also enjoyed seeing Ralph Howard and his family. It had been Ralph who took him under his wing, so to speak and had brought him into his family circle. It had been Ralph who taught him to use his past as a tool to carve a magnificent future for himself. He taught Sean how to love someone with all their frailties even when you do not like them or approve of what they do. This was Sean's saving grace as it allowed him to love his mother just as she was. It allowed him to not necessarily condone her behaviour -- for it is alright to hate the behaviour -- yet love the person. This also allowed him to not feel he needed to condone or accept the continuation of the behaviour in his life but he could "forgive and let live."

"I think ol' Ralph and his family are truly an example of spirituality" Sean thought to himself. "They deserve to have time to enjoy a great retirement if anyone does."

The noon news came on and the reporter who talked to him earlier was reporting on the lost boy Tommy Byers. "He is five years old with curly blonde hair. He is believed to be wearing a blue baseball cap, blue shorts, white and blue sweat shirt. He may or may not have runners on. This is a picture of Tommy at his sister's first birthday party. He is the young child in the background. His mother, stepdad and baby sister are in the foreground of the picture. We are now going to give a close up of Tommy's face. Anyone knowing anything about Tommy or his whereabouts is asked to call the RCMP Newton detachment or call the tip line."

Looking at the close up of Tommy it could have been a picture of Sean at that age. It was a little unnerving as the thought passed his mind. It was about that age that he too had been subjected to the "hardy party attitude" his own mother adopted for so many years. The parallels in his life and Tommy's were uncanny. His heart reached out to this little boy and then once again Sean had to keep himself in check as the emotional reminiscing did not serve either him or Tommy well at this time.

Just at the time Sean returned from his sentimental journey into the past, Leanne walked into the lunchroom. "See you at two," Leanne called to him, "We have all the crime scene pictures as well as Suzy, Brandon and I will have our paper work ready to discuss what we have learned and observed."

"It sounds great to me," Sean answered. "Help yourself to some fruit if you like. It's fresh from our favourite market."

"Thanks. I didn't get much of a breakfast this morning but my Dad handed me a bag of his famous muffins. I'll bring some to the meeting." Leanne said as she waved the open bag under Sean's nose and quickly snatched them back closing the bag in a playful motion to teasing his appetite.

Leanne had raised her twin boys on her own after her husband, another police officer had been killed in the line of duty. Her father had raised her after her mom had decided she did not want to be married anymore and left George with their eight year old daughter. George had to be both father and mother to Leanne and did a fantastic job of raising a beautiful caring girl into womanhood. Leanne's father George came to live with her to help raise the boys and once again George's skills as homemaker/cook had come in handy. Now that the boys were in their own law firm and had families of their own, Leanne and her Dad lived together going their own way as individuals but great company for each other at home. Often Leanne would say "I have a little house elf that cleans my house, tends my garden and bakes goodies to give my day a sweet treat."

"By the way Sean" Leanne said bring them back to the case at hand. "Dave Byers is flying in from Iran. He is on duty with our Canadian Arm Forces over there and is taking compassionate leave. He will be arriving here tomorrow at 4:45 a.m. and I have set an interview time for us to talk with him tomorrow at noon."

"Suzy and Brandon are interviewing the other family members now so we will have everything ready for the meeting at 2:00 p.m." Sean said as he cleaned up after himself and filled his coffee cup to take to his office with him.

Chapter 4

A voice came over the speaker in the conference room ... "Sergeant Fitzgerald, please come to reception."

Sean went into the public reception area and approaching Carrie, the receptionist, he asked, "Looking for me are you Carrie?" All six foot of him towered over her as she looked up into his sparkling blue eyes. Sean was the dream man of all the girls working in the office. It was no wonder, as he was a regular at the gym keeping his six-foot frame buffed. His sandy blonde, closely cropped, curly hair framed his Celtic facial features. Sean was always well dressed but most of all, he had a heart melting smile that gave him a boyish charm.

Carrie said "Yes ... a lady to see you. She would like to talk to you now if you have a moment. Her name is Joanna Lenardi. She's across the room standing looking out the window."

"Thanks Carrie," Sean gave her a warm smile and walked towards the woman at the window. He would have to be blind not to notice she was absolutely stunning. There she stood, silhouetted by the sun streaming through the window which gave her an almost angelic aura. She was dressed in a form fitting patty-green pant suit which flattered her petite, shapely body. Her long ravenous black hair fell in loose curls down her back and shone like silk.

There was something familiar about her Sean thought as he said "Excuse me? Ms. Lenardi?" As she turned, he realized this was the psychic who had called out to him as he entered the missing boy's home earlier today.

"Oh, hello Sergeant Fitzgerald," she said. Sean felt his heart leap inside his chest as she turned to face him. Her brown velvet eyes once more looked into his. "I was hoping to take a minute of your time to explain why I called out to you this morning."

Composed now to his professional demeanour Sean said, "Well frankly, Ms. Lenardi, I am really busy right now."

Then for some unknown reason he added, "but I can give you ten minutes so if you can help us ... great."

"What are you thinking?" Sean thought to himself as he ushered her into his office. Even knowing he must take every lead seriously no matter how slim. He still thought to himself, "This is an entire waste of time." Aloud he said "Please ... take this chair." He pulled out for her in front of the desk, "I hope you do not mind if I record our conversation Ms Lenardi."

"Not at all." she replied, as she sat in front of him at his desk "and please, call me Joanna." These words seemed to be soft and gentle as she quietly spoke to him. She looked deep into his eyes with each word she spoke, taking Sean a little further off guard. Not liking the feeling of not being totally in charge. Yet also feeling an underlying tranquillity that came with her very presence.

Quickly Sean brought himself back to the moment and to the subject at hand. "Well then Joanna ... what do you have that can help us in our investigation of this case?"

Joanna began to speak, "I had a dream this morning which I woke from about 3 a.m. A young boy about five years old came to me in the dream. He was dressed in blue pyjamas that had beige teddy bears printed on them and trailed a small teddy bear beside him that he held in his right hand. He was surrounded by a star-studded night sky and he was shining like a star as he himself was surrounded with a brilliant white aura. As I watched him move towards me, he said for me to ask about the wet pyjamas. I am not sure what that means but I know from past experiences that it must be significant in some way. Then when I put the news on this morning I saw the same little boy on the news. It was Tommy Byers."

"Did he say anything else?" Sean asked leaning slightly forward in his chair.

"No" Joanna replied. "But I may be able to help you further by linking back to Tommy's energy through a toy or walking through the home if that can be arranged. If you give me a call I can arrange a meeting with you or I could come to the house if you think the family would be alright with that and see what else I can pick up."

"I think for now the toy may be the best answer and less invasive to the family also less revealing to the general public or media to what we are doing. If you give me your phone number, I will call to arrange a meeting." Sean said.

"This is my business card," she said to Sean as she took out her business card. "I know you need to get as much information as you can as quickly as possible so if you would like to come to the centre this evening after my group has left. Around 9:30 p.m., then we could see what we can find out." Joanna stood up and passed her card to Sean. As her hand touched his, Sean was taken aback by the almost electric shock he experienced. "As a matter of fact if you chose to come for the meeting at 7 p.m. you may see what I do first hand, as I will be demonstrating spiritual facilitation this evening. You are more than welcome to attend as my guest."

Once more those brown velvet eyes seemed to draw him into a pool of emotions unlike anything he had experienced before and as Sean rose to his feet it was almost a dream-like feeling he experienced as he walked Joanna back to the reception area.

"Thank you for your time Sergeant Fitzgerald" Joanna said and extended her hand to Sean.

Sean took her hand and was barely able to discern what he himself was saying as he thanked her for coming in and told her he would call. With that Joanna was gone and Sean stood looking after her as she approached her car and drove away.

Carrie's voice brought him back to reality as she asked, "Shall I hold all calls while you are in your meeting Sean?"

"What? ... oh ... yes. Thank you Carrie. We will be through about 4 p.m. and I'll check with you then." Sean turned and headed for the meeting, still reeling from the strange affect Joanna seemed to have on him.

Chapter 5

Entering into the conference room Sean saw his whole team was already there and ready to go. Pulling out a chair at one end of the table he asked Suzy Wong to give her report as she was the first to talk to the mother.

Suzy read from her notes. "Mom says, the boy was in his bed when she looked in around six a.m. She gave the baby a bottle and went back to bed. At about nine a.m. the baby cried again and the father got up, took the child to the master bedroom to clean and change her before coming out for breakfast. Mom went to Tommy's room and he was missing. She seen he had wet the bed and became upset with him and went looking for him. Eventually she and the common-law husband realized the boy was not hiding and had vanished from the home. They checked neighbours and family to no avail. They had nowhere else to think to look. Later we checked some of the same places, checking with neighbours and family and we too came up empty. The dog handlers toured the neighbourhood after they thoroughly searched the house and home grounds. They too could not get a trail that lead anywhere. So we are at a dead end."

Brandon gave his report on the stepfather Don. "It appears that he has not too much to give us as he had not seen the boy since the night before when he put him in bed. It appears Don was quite upset with Marilyn the night before so although he had just a few beers with the guys prior to coming home it appears he made up for it and does not remember much of what went on at the party as he passed out on the bed just a few hours later. The party, according to the neighbours was still going strong at two am. One neighbour said it then quieted down enough that he went to sleep and did not really know if the party was over or whether a few stragglers remained behind when the others left. We also talked to other members of the family and have contacted most of the people from the party. No one had seen Tommy nor had any great insight to his whereabouts."

Leanne's turn came up and she brought forth the pictures taken in the boy's bedroom, the bathroom and other areas throughout the house. On Leanne's instruction the photographer took pictures from every angle possible. Working for many years as a crime scene photographer he knew his evidence was often critical to the case. His team marked and catalogued everything. The other forensic people were just as thorough. Leanne added "I have notes on my discussions with all parties and from a psychological standpoint; there are some that have me wanting to look deeper into what is going on in the family dynamics. The mother and stepdad are at the extreme opposite end of the emotional reactions so I think I may have to look deeper into their individual reactions to whether there is more than meets the eye here."

Sean nodded in agreement. "By the way did the forensic team say the bed was wet?" Sean asked.

"Yes. I felt the bed as well, and the bed linen was wet through to the mattress. Why do you ask Sean?" Leanne answered.

"Well in the pictures of the bedroom and the bathroom there were no pyjamas lying around. If this kid got up and changed into his clothes with the bedding still wet on the bed, no one had cleaned up the soiled linen so ... Where are the wet pyjamas?"

There are none in any of the pictures and I did not see any myself. I will check with the forensic team to see if they were in the clothes hamper and get back to you." Leanne reached for the inter-office phone and called the forensics department. "Hi Sarah. Leanne here. Did your team check the laundry hamper at the Byers home?"

"Hi Leanne. Yes we did and the clothes that were strewn on the laundry room. Why do you ask?" Sarah queried.

"We were wondering was there any wet pyjamas in the hamper that would have fit the five year old?" Leanne asked.

"There were a number of soiled pyjamas but none of the ones that size were still wet." Sarah replied. "The boy's bed was certainly soaked, so if the pyjamas were there they should have been pretty wet. A good question would be ... where are the wet pyjamas?"

"That's what Sean wants to know. Thanks Sarah. We will keep you posted. We'll talk soon, bye for now." Leanne turned to Sean and said "Hmm ... you have a good question there Sean. The obvious is often the thing we miss." Leanne then asked Sean, "What makes you think of about the pyjamas anyway?"

"The psychic who was outside of the house this morning, Joanna Lenardi, popped into my office for a chat. She told me about a dream or vision she had last night about a young boy who told her to ask about the wet pyjamas. Then in the morning she said she saw the picture of Tommy Byers on the amber alert. She realized he was the one who visited her in the night. She described the pyjamas so we need to ask the mother or better yet, Don about the pyjamas Tommy was wearing that night. Hopefully, without getting the wind up their sails about the pyjamas."

"The psychic ... hmm ... Now that is interesting is it not Sean?" Leanne replied with a little glint in her eye. "Did you see any smoke and mirrors?" she giggled.

"Okay! Okay! Have a good laugh. And here is a better one for you, I'm invited to go to her centre tonight. Want to come?" Sean partly wanted Leanne there too as he felt she would be able to help with the information and partly for a link to his own reality if he again had strange emotions rising up in Joanna's presence.

"Would love to come if only to be a 'fly on the wall' to observe your reactions to what these people do out there. If they can help us, in any way, then we are a head of the game." Leanne comment and asked, "What time do we meet?"

"If we want to attend the spiritual facilitation meeting we need to be there by 6:45. We will need to get a toy Tommy played with and bring it with us for Joanna. She will use it to link with the boy, she says. If you can't make it for 6:45 p.m. you can join me for the private meeting at 9:30 p.m. with Joanna." Then Sean added, "I'll give you the address."

"No need for the address. The twins and their friends have told me about this centre and I looked into it a few years back although this will be the first time I will have attended the actual meeting. It should be very interesting, in more ways than one." Leanne teased him with a knowing wink. "As I told you, I am still open to the possibilities but look at you, old sceptical friend of mine. Have you changed your total concept on your psychic ... smoke and mirror theory?"

"Not yet" Sean answered, "but this thing with the pyjamas has stimulated my curious mind. If she had a dream with Tommy asking her to ask us about the wet pyjamas and it turns out they have not been found then that could open up a whole new line of questioning And definitely a direction that would, certainly point to someone at the house knowing more than they are telling us. It also would have me convinced that there may be some validity to this psychic stuff." Sean turned as he turned away from the coffee machine to asked "Should I pick you up tonight?"

"No. I'll meet you there. As I have shopping to do for my God-daughter's baby shower before I go anywhere tonight." Then as Leanne started to leave the room she came back and asked "Do you want me to pick up a toy from Tommy's Mom? I could find out the description of pyjamas Tommy had on as well."

Sean nodded "Good idea," and added "Make up some story like we may need the toy for the dogs to pick up the scent. We do not want to let anyone know what we are doing just yet."

"Fair enough. See you later at the centre." And with that Leanne left for to do her errands before going home.

Chapter 6

Arriving home, Sean parked his Chrysler 300 in the driveway of his townhouse. He always liked to have his cars and his home, not only comfortable, but practical for his needs. His one level 2 bdrm. plus den town-home offered great indoor and outdoor living. Outside patios to entertain in the balmy evenings and quality finished interior accented with comfortable, quality furnishings. The foyer with crown mouldings, a crystal chandelier and matching wall sconces. French doors to the main part of the home, welcome him as he entered. The remainder of his home reflected a quality yet practicality for a single man's needs. Many of the wives of his close male friends comment on how well kept his home is and asked how he could possibly keep it so tidy and clean. His secret, he told them, was he was lazy.

"How can you say you're lazy" his best friend's wife Marny had said, when she dropped in to pick up her husband Dan one Sunday afternoon. "I know you had company last night and today you went golfing with my husband and your place looks immaculate."

"I am lazy though," Sean confirmed, "I hate spending hours and hours cleaning up so I put away what I take out as soon as I am finished with it and also make sure I keep no junk mail, papers, once I have looked at it I recycle it. That way I clean up after myself as I go instead of saving it for a specific day. Doesn't seem such a big chore that way either."

"Maybe I'll give that a try. Sounds really good to me, however, I need to get Dan and the rest of the family to buy into the plan." Marny said, with a roll of her eyes and a look that told Sean she didn't think it would work at her house.

Heading straight for his bedroom, Sean opened his closet where, like the rest of his home, was a perfectly organized display of his wardrobe. Colour coordinated dress slacks and shirts, a shelf with sweaters and t-shirts, socks and shoes in their organizers. The closet was cedar lined and left a fresh air scent on his clothes. His taste leaned to the light and casual wear for the most part, reflecting Sean's personality. One end of his closet there was his more formal wear including his red serge official uniform of the RCMP that he wore for special occasions.

After deciding to wear beige dress slacks with a matching shirt, brown corduroy jacket and brown, highly polished leather loafers, Sean headed for the shower.

It was so relaxing to just let the warm water run over his body and feel the tensions of the day leave his tired muscles. Sean found himself humming a song his father use to sing to his mother so many years ago. "The Rose of Tralee."

Sean's father, Daniel Fitzgerald was well known in the town. He and his wife, Mary Rose, came from in Ireland. As a great singer, Daniel was nicked named 'Danny Boy.' Even after coming to Canada, Daniel Fitzgerald could be found each weekend singing and playing in the local pubs. His band Danny Boy and the Celtic Wanderers would pack people in to hear their version of the popular Irish songs, especially on St. Patrick's Day.

How wonderful those younger years were ... before the accident on the construction site where Danny Boy worked his day job. The scaffolding collapsed and in that split second in time, Sean's life was changed from a happy childhood with loving parents to a life of being dragged from one town to another by a mother, who could not really get handle on things after her world came crashing down. She was always looking for something to dull the pain of the loss of the love of her life and often that was Irish whiskey along with the arms of a string of lovers. Some she may have for one night or maybe she would join up with some of them for months at a time. Sean had no choice when they had to pick up a move. Sean thought, as he shampooed his hair, "One year I was in three schools in three different cities."

Even so, Mary Rose was his mother and he loved her dearly. There had been times when she had tried to stay sober and make a better life for Sean but then it was waitress work and long hours and most months not enough money to pay the rent, food and other things they needed. When the pressure got too great, Mary Rose would drop into the pub on the way home just for one drink. Those were the nights Sean hated the most as he never knew who would be in bed with his mother the next morning.

It wasn't too often he visited the darker side of his past as he long ago had learned not to go to there in his memories. It served no purpose.

Sean, however, still chose to return to those happier, positive days when he heard or sung the old songs his father sang to Mary Rose Fitzgerald on those nights so long ago. Mary Rose and Danny Boy sat out on the porch swing with Sean curled up beside them. Young as he was, Sean could feel the love they had for each other and for him. "When I find the right woman for me, that's how it is going to be" Sean thought as he rubbed his body dry. "It is not easy to find couples today, who have that type of appreciation for each other but Sean was still hopeful that the special someone would come when the time was right."

Then to his complete surprise, he started to wonder what kind of wife Joanna Lenardi would make. "Where is that thought coming from?" Sean asked himself right out loud. "Give your head a shake Sean ... you're living in a dream world if you think that could ever be a possibility. Your worlds are so far apart ... you would never agree on anything to do with the psychic world for starters." None the less, Sean could not stop the excitement that the thought of Joanna brought to him as he felt the awareness of sexual attraction for Joanna surging through his whole being.

The shrill ring of his front door buzzer brought him back to the everyday world with a jolt. Sean wrapped a thick terry-towel bathrobe around himself and discovered it was Leanne at the door.

Once inside Leanne said, "I have Tommy's favourite toy, a police car. I brought it over as I have to back out on going to the Joanna's demonstration with you tonight." Leanne lamented. "I'm on my way to see my God-daughter in hospital and I have to find out what is going on. Her husband is so upset he isn't making any sense on the phone. I have to run but good luck tonight. I want a full report in the morning."

"Hope it's nothing serious with your God-daughter. I'll be waiting to hear about her prognosis as well. If you need some compassionate leave or if I can help in any way just let me know."

"Thanks Sean," Leanne replied, "I will know more after I meet with the family and see how things are going."

"I will miss your support tonight though. I'm still not sure about this psychic stuff but you can bet I will be giving you a full report in the morning." Taking the toy car from Leanne, Sean added, "The story Joanne tells from this toy will be more than interesting, especially if any of it proves out to be information she can't know about Tommy's disappearance through normal channels and if it is valid information that helps us locate him."

"That would make a believer out of you if she was able to find him wouldn't it?" Leanne asked Sean. "I know I would be sold on her abilities if we could find Tommy from her directing us to where he is." Then she added, "Oh by the way, Tommy was wearing blue PJ's with brown teddy bear print. Makes one go hmm, doesn't it? " Giving Sean a wink Leanne prepares to leave saying, "See you in the morning. Have a great night."

With that Sean opened the door and Leanne headed for her car.

Chapter 7

Meanwhile, after leaving the RCMP detachment office, Joanna Lenardi headed home to prepare her centre for the 'Evening of Mediumistic Demonstration'. It was only two hours away and she had to have supper before going to the sanctuary.

Joanna found Sergeant Sean Fitzgerald an extremely pleasant and sincere young man, who had a passion for his work. "Not too hard to look at either." Joanna thought to herself. A little giggle emerged out loud at that thought.

Joanna and two of her students, who are going to join her as the spiritual facilitators for the evening, Julie Strand and Lorna Kidder, came in together with hellos and hugs. "Is there anything we can do Joanna?" Julie asked.

"Yes. If you two could get the coffee and goodies ready for the evening tea, I would appreciate it." Joanna answered. "I have had a busy day." She did not share her events of the day for if one of the girls picked up something for Sean, Joanna wanted it to be fresh and without influence. It would be more evidential that way, for Sean, for Joanna and her students.

"It is a lovely day." Lorna commented, "Your property is always a pleasure to see as each season has its own beauty." Then she added "It is as if each time I come here I'm returning home. Maybe that is what I like best in working with the Spirit world; wonderful people on both sides." then giving Joanna a smile, she and Julie started to move towards the kitchen area.

Joanna left and entered into the residential part of the building to prepare herself for the evening. "I need to get a little quiet time before the evening's event so if I take a quick shower and have a light supper. That should allow me time in the meditation garden before others start coming through the grounds." She thought to herself.

Chapter 8

Sean pulled up in front of the address on Joanna's card to find he was sitting in front of ten acre estate. A hanging sign at the entrance to the grounds said, "The Haven of Prosperity." The front yard was landscaped with multi level terraced gardens. In the left corner of the front garden of the property a huge, story high boulder, with a statue of an angel carrying a pitcher sitting at the very highest point. A never-ending flow of water poured out from the pitcher to feed the man-made stream, weaving its way through the top level, creating waterfalls, as it careened over the rockeries from one level to the next. On the lowest level the water settled into a crystal clear pond. This pond became a "wishes and prayer pond." Many people had thrown coins into the pond along with their prayer or wish. A sign read "Donations from this pond help our local food bank. We thank you for caring."

Many sculptured birds and animals were posed around the pond. Some posed quenching their thirst, grazing on the well manicured lawn while others looking up in the direction of the entrance to the gardens. Sean felt as if they were welcoming him as he pulled into a parking space in the sanctuary's parking lot.

"There must be some big money in this psychic business," he thought, then chastising himself for his cynical attitude. Leanne had done a background check on Joanna and told him "She's as clean as the fresh driven snow Sean. She has no complaints or criminal activity of any kind." Of course this did not give him any insight into anything else he maybe would like to know about this fascinating lady, who seems to have some strange affect on his emotions.

A sign at on the sanctuary entrance to the main building invited the visitors who arrive early to enjoy the gardens and to feel free to rest and absorb the beauty of God's creations. Sean looked at his watch and realized he was a half hour early and decided to accept the invitation and strolled down a pathway.

The gardens, at the back of the home, were well kept but had a look and feel of being kept the way nature had intended the land to be. Many of the large trees had been kept as the mainstay of the garden's design where others were planted with a definite design in mind. Pathways lead away from the main building to other restful spots throughout the acreage.

Trellised archways allowed for a variety of climbing flowers and fruits to grace different garden entrances. Fruit trees, herb and vegetable gardens as well as small orchards, with green spaces with some offered benches to sit and enjoy the quietness. Some picnic areas both open and under cover for the visitors who choose to share a meal with one another may gather. Another sign on the main pathway invited the visitors to partake of the bountiful harvest from the prosperity gardens and trees. Both drinking fountains to quench the thirst of the visitors, bird baths so they may watch the birds play and be refreshed. Sean soon realizes this was a place of peacefulness and had that essence of tranquillity he felt in Joanna's presence earlier this afternoon.

Sean was totally surprised how he was letting go of the day's pressures in this place. "This must be what people imagine heaven is like." Sean thought to himself and settled into the natural rhythm of the song birds, the gentle breezes and the sweet smells of the grasses and flowers. He leaned back against the bench ... closed his eyes ... until ...a light touch of a hand on his shoulder ... and soft voice speaking his name jolted him back into his consciousness.

He knew even before he turned around that it was Joanna. Once more he was captured by those eyes as he turned and looked upward at Joanna who stood behind him. "So glad you could join us Sergeant. I hope you have enjoyed our gardens." Joanna said.

"Yes, thank you for allowing me to experience the peacefulness you have here. It is not often I get a chance to just sit in such complete stillness." Sean said as he rose to greet her.

"I am pleased you took time to enjoy God's handy work, if only for a little while." Joanna said with sincerity. "Feel free to drop by anytime you feel the need. I am just on my way back from my meditation garden to go into the sanctuary. Please, join me and we can both enjoy the walk back together." With that she gave him a smile, linked her arm in his and they walked silently along the pathway back to the Sanctuary.

Chapter 9

Joanne had excused herself at the entrance to the Sanctuary and told Sean she would see him after the program was over. Opening the door Sean was surprised to find the Sanctuary was a reflection of the outside gardens with a stone garden wall part way up and glassed walls and ceiling as the enclosure that allowed the sky and outside light to add to the feeling of openness and oneness. At the front was a raised platform with comfortable garden type chairs placed amidst trees, plants and flowers. At the very back of the platform was a pool formed of natural rocks which, like the outside pond, it had an Angel holding a pitcher with continually flowing water pouring into the pond below. There were two rostrums for speakers, a pipe organ, grand piano and an area for the musicians and choirs. Two steps down, level with the audience, was another area that was clear of anything other than an alter and beautiful vegetation. The ground level floor was a made from flagstones so chairs, draped with white linen seat covers, could be safely placed in rows. The flagstone floor allowed for frequent pressure washing, keeping its pristine appearance.

The auditorium was over three-quarters full when Sean entered and he chose a seat closest to the entrance door to be able to view both the demonstrators and the audience. "There must be a hundred and fifty people here." Sean commented to himself which meant the sanctuary held about two hundred people. "This must be a pretty prosperous business, no wonder it is named 'The Haven of Prosperity'." He leaned back, folded his arms and waited for the program to start.

About five minutes later an announcement came over the PA system for everyone to please come into the sanctuary. As they did, almost every remaining seat was taken.

At the microphone a man in his early forties greeted everyone "Hi, I'm Rod Blake ... and I am your chairperson for this evening. Could you **please** check that your communications devices are turned off. We only want messages from the other side this evening." He teased with a big smile. A big laugh from the crowd rang out. He continued on with "You are in for a fabulous evening of fun and learning as Joanna Lenardi and two of her senior students bring us a Demonstration of Mediumship. A little request that we have of you is that if one of the ladies speak to you that you answer her. You can imagine that if you tried to phone a friend and they just nodded, you would have great trouble in knowing if they are there or if they are hearing you. So ... big smiles and big voices." Now without further delay give a big hand for Joanna Lenardi and her fellow demonstrators ... Julie Strand and Lorna Kidder."

The applause thundered out as Joanna and the two other ladies took the stage.

Joanna stepped up to the front of the platform and addressed the crowd while the other two took seats at opposite sides of the stage. "Good evening."

"Good evening Joanna," they replied in unison. The room filled with sudden electricity as each person sat up just a little bit straighter in the chairs.

"We are so glad to be able to be here tonight to facilitate your family and friends from spirit. We know they are just a thought away and we link with love to the other side, where life is a continuum." Joanna was looking around the room yet it felt as if she is addressing each person individually.

When she would find the area she was looking for Joanna continued, "I would like to come to the couple in the third row over here ... "

"Thank you Joanna." the young man answered as he held the young woman's hand tightly in his hands.

As everyone looked over in the direction of a young couple in their mid twenties, Joanna continued on. "I have a little girl ... about four years old coming in for you ... she tells me to say that you are the "bestest" mommy and daddy ever ... she says she has met 'Uppa' picking strawberries in his garden. Uppa says to tell you he is looking after me and we are going to make a pretty garden for when you come to see us. He says to tell you that he has both his feet again and he can run fast with me on his shoulders like he use to do when I was two." The young mother grabbed hold of her husband and began to sob, "Mommy don't cry ... I have no more needles or people poking my stomach ... I can run and play now. I see you everyday looking at my baby book and that is good 'cause it's our time together ... but don't be sad" Joanna continued on, "Remember to love baby Jimmy as much as you love me ... Love you mommy and daddy ... love you." Joanna added "she blows you kisses as she runs back to the gentleman in the garden."

Sean could see the emotional response to the message that Joanna had given them but then ... "Maybe she may already knows them and their situation," he thought to himself being the sceptical person he, is he would need to know it was not a set up like he has seen in those training tapes on scam artists and con men.

The young father gathered his emotions together and said "Thank you Joanna. Our young daughter died last week after being in cancer treatment for two years. 'Uppa' is my Dad. Mary-Margret named him that as the first words she spoke to him was 'Up Pa ... up Pa'. He would put her on his shoulders and run with her down the garden path. My father's diabetes took his left foot, his leg and eventually his life. Thank you, thank you for telling us our daughter is with my dad and that they are alive in spirit." The young couple hugged and cried together and Joanna looked towards her student Julie Strand who rose up and moved forward. Julie addressed an older couple in their late sixties sitting half way back in the sanctuary. "May I come to you?" she asked.

"Yes ... thank you." the woman answered.

There is a young woman with you who tells me she is a teacher. She says she loved to teach. She still is teaching. She laughs and says the first year as her children left her to go to the next grade she came home and cried but each time the new year brought new joys and new challenges. She had to let the children go each year and open her heart to the new ones coming in. She says you are having a hard time letting her go and have not gone on with your lives as you should. She tells me she feels it is time for you to move on with your lives. She says to you now, "Live well ... be all you can be ... for in living well you honour me." Again the people receiving the message response validated the message being completely understood.

Sean became more intrigued and then Joanna addressed him directly by his first name. "I have a man here who came in singing 'Oh Danny Boy' and says that Danny Boy actually has another meaning for you, other than the song itself. He is quite the singer. Now he is singing "The Rose of Tralee." He is a tall man not much different to you in appearance and I feel a father link here. He says your mother is also with him and they both watch over you now. Mother is saying she is sorry she was not the mother she should have been for you but she and your father are proud of the man you are today. She says they love you and are saving a seat on the garden swing for you."

With that Sean felt the memory return to his experience earlier today in the shower. You would have thought that Joanne had bugged his apartment ... or was able to read his thoughts even when she is not in his presence. He heard himself say, "Thank you." to Joanna for the message even though he felt more like an observer than a participant at this moment ... feeling a little detached from reality as his father and mother were described in such a way he could not doubt there was a contact with something outside of Joanna's own self as she had no way of knowing these things of herself even if she did extensive research this was not common knowledge one could access.

After a number of other messages that all seemed to have great meaning to the recipients the program was over.

Once more the young gentleman chairing for the evening moved to the microphone.

"Thank you for joining us tonight and please join me in a closing prayer and join us for coffee and conversation." Rod Blake said.

After the closing prayer Joanna and her entourage moved down the aisle towards the reception area followed by the audience. Sean followed the people into a reception area, where they helped themselves to beverages and fresh baked sweet goods.

The excitement of those who had received messages and a willingness to share the experience of hearing from a loved one had the place buzzing. By just listening to the people sharing the full story like the young couple with the four year old daughter in spirit, most of the people, who received messages, were there for the first time, just as he was. It was very evident that there was no way the demonstrators could know the particulars of the lives of these people. They were strangers until tonight.

After a few minutes and some pleasant conversation Sean looked up to see Joanna coming towards him. She extended her hand out to take his and said "Come with me. We can go to my meditation garden and talk awhile about young Tommy." Then as they walked along she asked "Were you able to bring a personal item of Tommy's with you?"

"Yes, I have it here." and he took the toy police car from the bag he was carrying. "He apparently wants to be a police man when he grows up; hope he can be." Sean continued.

"We have to believe we will find him and bring him home safely at this point of the investigation and give our prayers ... our energy of intent to him returning home." Joanna said softly to Sean.

Joanna linked her arm into Sean's arm once more and they wandered mist the gardens now lit with twinkling lights in the trees and solar powered pathway lights to guide the way back to the Meditation Garden.

It was a silent walk but one full of feelings too complicated to even understand. That mixed feeling of tranquility and excitement surging through Sean's veins made him wish he had met Joanna under different circumstances.

Sean had a job to do and he knew he would need to keep a professional aura about himself. So he commanded himself to stay professional in his thinking. Get the job done and bring Tommy home.

Chapter 10

Back at the Detachment in Surrey other things have been happening. Constable Suzy Wong had contacted the Canadian Arm Forces to notify Tommy's biological father, David Byers, of his son's disappearance. David Byers was serving in the Middle East and had no idea of what was going on at home. Suzy received a fax from Dave Byers' Commanding Officer to say David Byers was being flown home and would arrive in the early morning. They said he would be transported to them at the detachment after he arrived. Suzy called Leanne who thanked her for the message and said she was in contact with Sean about the meeting with Tommy's father.

Leanne had been at the hospital with her God-daughter and the emergency had now had a positive outcome. The doctors decided to do a C-section and although quite small and needing to have special care, the babies seemed to be holding their own nicely. Leanne had just left the happy couple looking through the glass at the two miracles, one boy ... one girl, that now were in their charge.

Leanne had just stepped into her own car when she heard from Suzy Wong. "I better text Sean," she thought to herself and after doing so headed home to catch a short nap. The text read ..."Dave Byers will arrive at Chilliwack Armed Forces Base and be brought in from there."

Leanne would meet with Sean for 4:30 a.m. at the detachment so they could be sure the father was given all the information they could give him regarding his son's disappearance. Leanne's big motherly heart just ached for this young sailor, who was travelling with a heart full of pain ... not knowing whether his young son was dead or alive.

Leanne now turned her thoughts to Sean. "Wonder how he made out at the centre and if Joanna was able to get any further information." Such a simple thing yet so easy to overlook, the wet pyjamas had created quite a dilemma in the minds of all of the people working on the case. If he wet the bed, got up and changed into his day clothes and left on his own accord, then "Where are the wet pyjamas?" Had someone picked up the soiled pyjamas? Wouldn't it be logical to think they would surely strip the linen from the bed if they took time to clean up?" Or not pick up at all, which would be more in keeping with a family in turmoil about a missing child. They would not, in Leanne's thinking, even be thinking of the soiled linen or clothing, just getting help for the lost child.

Leanne pulled up in front of her home and as she stepped out of the car realized just how tired and hungry she really was. "It's a Hard Day's Night" she hummed to herself as she related the old favourite song, to her own day.

"Has it really only been one day?" Leanne asked herself as she put the key into the front door lock. "Honey I'm home" Leanne called out and her yellow lab rose up from the doggy bed, beside the fireplace in the den, coming to greet her. "Good dog, Jessie-Jane. I always can count on you to be here whatever time I come home. Good dog, good dog." She snuggled close playfully with her loving pet.

Going into the kitchen Leanne had seen a note on the fridge. "Hi darlin' girl ... hope you had a great day. I left you some of my meat and potato pie in the fridge ... if you are hungry and some tarts for dessert ... baking powder biscuits for you and Sean for mornin' as I know without ya tellin' me, it's been another long day. Love ya me darling girl ... have a good sleep ... Love Dad.
PS Gone to Poker night at McGee's"

"Good old Dad," Leanne said to herself. "I am so lucky to have a little house elf who takes such good care of me." Opening the fridge, "A bit late for the meat and potato pie, dad, but Oh! Oh! Oh! Those lemon tarts sure will do the trick." Leanne balanced one on top of another, closed the fridge and headed to the table. Clicking the kettle into the heat position, she waited for her good cup of Irish breakfast tea before devouring the lemon treat. "How sweet life is," she thought as she enjoyed a moment to reflect on the new babies who arrived a little ahead of schedule.

"So good. Thank you God! Even though there was a need of an emergency C-section, mom and babies are fine." As always, Leanne's gratitude for her father's good health, having him still such an active part of her life, was a silent prayer she said each night. So tonight as she sat in silence her heart was full and her spirit energized.

"I am truly blessed." Leanne thought to herself, as she jumped into the shower, promising the body a long leisurely bath soon. "Morning will be here all too soon." She thought as the water soothed her tired bones.

As she got into bed Leanne thought once more of poor David Byers who was heading home to God knows what. Then snuggled down into her warm bed, she prayed "God send your angels to help him on this journey that must seem like it will to never end." Leanne then rolled on her side, pulled up the covers up around her neck and fell into a deep sleep.

Chapter 11

Joanna and Sean sat in the glassed in gazebo in the centre of the Meditation Garden. White wicker furniture with white and large green leaf printed, heavily padded cushions, glass table topped wicker tables and again the outside garden carried on into the gazebo through the glassed in enclosure. Flagstone floors and inset solar lighting that was triggered by the level of natural light and came on as needed. Outside and inside floral plants and small trees adorned the spaces to give that garden like essence that was the theme throughout the estate.

Once more Sean was taken by the artistic and practicality of the whole property. "This must have cost a fortune to build, much less its ongoing maintenance expenses." He thought to himself but before he could ponder further he heard Joanna ask him to have a seat.

"Would you like some Ice tea?' Joanna asked. She opened the under counter bar fridge and brought out the large pitcher of tea, then placed it on the glass tray on the table and in response to Sean's answer, poured a tall frosted glass full of tea and passed it to him.

Curling up in the wicker loveseat Joanna reach over and picked up the toy police car. She switched on her tape machine and sat back, then closed her eyes. There were a few minutes of silence before Joanna began to speak.

"I see young Tommy in the bedroom. He has pulled the covers up over his head. He is holding a small brown teddy bear and squeezing it tighter and tighter as if the bear can shut off the angry voices.

"I hear him call out someone's name ... 'Daddy Don ... ' it sounds like to me. He gets out of bed and runs down the hall and calls to someone 'Don't hit Daddy Don ... Don't hit Daddy Don ... ' and he is pulling at a man's jacket. The man is turned away from me so I cannot see his face" then Joanna said "I see a woman's hands grabbing Tommy and shaking him ... '*Smarten up*' she says, as she all but drags him down the hall to his room and flings him onto his bed. I feel a thump on the back of my head and then nothing. It is obvious that in the anger the person throwing him onto the bed was not aware he hit his head. This was a serious blow ... not an intentional act of harming the child but the result of an action in anger without regard for the consequences. The time was about 2:30 a.m. when I feel his physical presence left this home. His body, however, was moved some time after that..."

"You sense that he is dead then Joanna?" Sean queried.

"Wish I could say otherwise, but I fear he is not with us in this physical world. I could be wrong and he is just unconscious and I'm not able to communicate the difference from him. As it is at this particular time I am linking with his out of body experience." After a short silence Joanna asked "By the way ... did you find the wet pyjamas?"

Sean replied "No! We didn't find them so far. We do know the description of the pyjamas you gave is accurate though. " Sean really did not want to hear the answer he felt was coming, when he asked, "Do you think they took him somewhere else to hide the body still in the pyjamas?"

"I think so. That is how he first appeared ... in the pyjamas. So there must be great significance to the pyjamas relating with what has happened to him." Joanna replied. "It will be important in discerning the truth to what has actually happened to him."

After another moment of silence Joanna said "I am going to try and get him to show me the surrounding area where his physical body is now. He has a spiritual body and can zone in on the physical one." Joanna explained. "He is now protected in the spirit world and has no fear of what is going on here in our world but he does want to help you, Sergeant Fitzgerald, with your investigation he wants everyone to know what has happened to him."

Joanna leaned back once more and closed her eyes. "I see an area on the Fraser River where they load and unload cargo from ships. I can see a man ... dressed in a seaman's pea jacket, jeans and navy toque. He has a canvass bag over his shoulder. It is dark and he is walking towards one of the ships. It is about 5:30 a.m. Now he's running up the gang plank, looking over his shoulder and disappears in the darkness. The ship has big double T's in the name." Joanne goes quiet again and then says "Sorry that is all I can see at this time. This is the problem with my work; we often get jigsaw pieces to put together. We will hope a few more pieces fall into place over the next few days."

"Thank you for all you are doing to help. I will call you tomorrow, if I may, just to keep in touch." Inwardly Sean really did not want this night to end and was glad there was a reason to keep in touch. "If you receive any more impressions or information do not hesitate to call me, personally, if I have not checked in with you."

Sean stood up and handed her his card with his home number added to the other information. As their hands touched once more, Sean had a surge of excitement run through his very being. "Call my cell and if no answer, call my home number." Inwardly he hoped that she would hold on to the number and call whether there was anything new or not. Sean wished they had met under different circumstances but for now, he reminded himself, Tommy is the top priority and he was not allowed to let his personal feelings interfere with doing his job.

Joanna got up from her chair and moved with him towards the doorway. "I'll walk back with you." She said "It is such a beautiful night and I always love it when there is someone to appreciate the moonlit gardens with me."

Just as Sean opened the door for Joanna, he felt his phone vibrate. "Excuse me, Joanna, this may be important." It was important, as it was Leanne texting with a message about young Tommy's natural father.

Once Sean had read the message and pocketed his phone Joanna moved towards him. She linked her arm through his as she walked him back to his car in the parking lot. The walk in the moonlight, through the gardens, lent another whole romantic aura to the evening and Sean felt somewhat disappointed when he seen his car, just a few steps away.

"Well now Sergeant," Joanna said as she released her arm from his "Here is your car." Sean moved into the driver's seat leaving the window open, resting his one arm on the sill. Joanna placed her hand on his and added "May angels go with you and lead you where you need to go." Then she turned, walking through the rose arbour to the lower entrance to the residence.

Sean watched until she was out of sight then started the car. Knowing he had to keep his mind on the task at hand, as a young boy's life may hang in the balance, Sean brought himself back to the reality of why he was with Joanna. What Joanna had picked up from the toy police car did not sound too promising for the safe return of Tommy Byers. She did say that he could be unconscious and out of the body though, so this gave him some hope the boy may be alive.

"Who was the man with the duffle bag and what does he have to do with Tommy? If it is any connection at all to the case who knows? Was Tommy in the duffle bag? If so, was he dead or alive? We can only pray that he is alive somewhere." Sean thought to himself.

Sean arrived at his townhouse he parked in his garage and sent a message to Leanne. "Will have coffee ready ... see you at 4:30 a.m. ... any chance Dad baked something good to have with the coffee?"

"It has been a busy day." he thought to himself. One filled with more questions than answers especially about how Joanna could know all those things about his own father and mother. He certainly had not mentioned anything about his own personal life to her nor for that matter to too many other people either. Probably his only confidant had been Ralph Howard and his wife. He had not shared this part of himself with his now partner Leanne with whom he shared most of his life, as he knew he was completely safe and protected by her as a partner and friend. Even so, he had not brought his pain to her table. "It is a little unnerving, to say the least that a perfect stranger can know so much about your hidden secrets without knowing you at all." Sean thought as he opened the door to the townhouse. "From what I witnessed tonight I need to know more about this psychic stuff and maybe not be so quick to dismiss it as 'hokey pokey, sham scam.'"

Chapter 12

Sean found himself quite restless in bed. The day had been a long one. You would think he would drop off to sleep as soon as his head hit the pillow but his mind would not shut off. The day had held a load of conflicting thoughts. One minute convinced that all this ability to communicate with the dead was bunk, to the next minute convinced that someone does not just pull the fact about the wet pyjamas, people's deceased child or facts like "Danny Boy" out of a hat as lucky guesses. Joanna seems to be a genuine person, who has an ability that she uses to help others but then there is that elaborate estate and the cost of building maintenance it must take a small fortune for upkeep. Is she using people's grief and sadness in some way, building their trust and confidence in her and then bilking them for money with the other hand, to fund her elaborate life style. Does she get people dependent on her emotionally and then solicit funds from these poor emotionally crippled souls? Not too different than the old gypsy scams, that wins confidence in the readings they do and then draw people into solutions she can offer, for a price.

Sean thought to himself that it is hard to believe that Joanne fits into a scammer's category when there was this overwhelming feeling of warmth and excitement that comes over him in her presence, giving him a feeling of belonging and being loved that Sean had not experienced for many years. Yes, and a feeling of being able to trust this woman, not something Sean did easily. All of these mixed up emotions ran through his mind. "I'm usually a good judge of character" Sean said to himself "but I feel like I can't really figure this lady out."

It was not that easy to let go of Joanna, however. Her face and those hypnotic brown eyes seemed to play on his mind each time he closed his eyes. "Not the worse thoughts to take you to dreamland" Sean finally said to himself as he turned over puffing his pillow into a comfortable position and soon was dreaming of the wonderful walk they took in the moonlight until the alarm brought him quickly into the reality of a new day. "Best get on my horse" Sean said to himself if he was to get to the office ahead of Leanne and have things ready for the boy's father's visit.

Sean moved his car through the quiet streets. Even most of the hardiest of party goers are home at 3:30 a.m. so the streets were almost deserted. Pulling up to the stationhouse Sean saw Leanne step from her car in the next parking spot

"Hi Sean. Scones and lemon tarts for breakfast, compliments of my Dad. May not be the most nutritional or conventional breakfast food but definitely delicious." Leanne teased as they both walked toward the door that led to the reception area. "Had a call from Chilliwack Armed Forces Base that Dave Byers arrived in a few minutes ago and they will transport him here to us, so that will save some time for everyone. How do you want to handle this Sean? The father knows very few details of what has gone on here so we will need to get him up to speed with what we know."

"I think it would be good to have him in one of the lounge rooms so we can make him as comfortable as possible. The interrogation rooms are a little cold and using one of our offices will also seem a little less than empathetic for the pain he is going through at this time." Sean was more or less asking for input from Leanne than making a hard and fast decision so he asked Leanne "What do you think?

Leanne nodded an approval "Good idea Sean" she replied and once in the lounge started setting the coffee tray and lemon tarts, her dad made, on a coffee table that could be reach easily from the leather sofa and the two matching chairs setting in the corner by the window.

"This is really one of the parts of our job that is the hardest." Leanne stated. "I can't help relating with the parents and feel heartbroken for them but also there is a part of me that says 'Thank God it's not my child who is missing.'"

Both Sean and Leanne were quiet for a few moments and then Leanne added "I do take comfort in knowing that we are here to do this job and are here to see the families are treated with the loving compassion that they need."

"We do the best we can Leanne. When we bring one child home safe and sound, that's a good day. Let's hope it is a good day for Tommy." Sean showed his venerable side for just a brief moment with his facial expressions showing his inner feelings. Leanne had seen it many times before so she was not surprised that this big, strong, no nonsense guy had a heart as big as the whole outdoors.

Sean was paged to come to reception and as he did he saw a young naval Petty Officer standing looking visibly shaken. He looked like he had been beaten, as if he had just come out of the worst battle one could imagine.

Extending his hand to the young man Sean spoke softly, "Mr. Byers, I am Sergeant Sean Fitzgerald. Please come with me to the lounge down the hall."

Both Dave Byers and Sean were quiet until they arrived in the room and Sean introduced Leanne and asked Dave to have a seat. Once seated, Dave Byers asked Sean to give him the details about his son's disappearance. "I need to know exactly what has happened and if you have any leads about where he is or what I can do to help." Dave was shaking and emotionally drained from what he did not know and Sean knew it was going to be worse for him as he and Leanne told him what they did know.

After fully realizing the situation his son had been in prior to the disappearance, what was left of the colour in Dave Byers' face drained away and left a contrast of white skin and jet black short cropped hair. His blue eyes sunken into the sockets from the tears he had shed and the lack of sleep. "I tried to get custody of my son but because I am in the navy I can be shipped out at anytime, so the courts felt he was best with his mother. What kind of woman is she anyway, certainly can't call her a mother?" Dave was now becoming agitated and angry to add to his frustration. He had wanted to be there for his son but legally and the distance he was from home made it impossible to keep a close eye on Marilyn and her treatment of their son.

God knows whether the son he loved so dearly is alive, full of fear somewhere or maybe dead already. Sean brushed the thought from his mind and tried to replace it with something positive to say when Dave started to talk once more.

"I need to talk to Marilyn," Dave said "and to that 'Boy Toy' she has living with her. They must know more than they are telling." The tone of Dave's voice was that of a man ready to challenge Marilyn and Don.

"How about we get you some rest first. The reclining leather chairs here serve as emergency beds for us many nights when we are unable to go home. We have showers in the locker room. Sergeant Chatman and I will bring both Marilyn and Don here to talk with you and with us in the morning. It will be better for all of you as we will be here to act as a buffer for the emotions that are bound to be running high at the moment." Sean said, as he moved towards the storage closet pulling out a blanket. "It is five a.m. so let's say we will call you at seven-thirty. You can get a shower and some breakfast before we bring them here for eight thirty in the morning to answer some of your questions." Then Sean added, placing a hand on Dave's shoulder "You will do a lot better if you can get some sleep as you are not going to be of any use to us -- your son or yourself -- if you are so exhausted. You can't think straight with emotional and physical exhaustion."

"I know you're right Sergeant Fitzgerald," Dave replied "but I don't think I can sleep."

"That's okay, try and rest anyway." Sean said. He and Leanne left the room and not two minutes later, Dave Byers was sound asleep. Nature has its own way of making the body give in when it has had all it can take.

Chapter 13

Constable Suzy Wong had to go to the house to pick up Marilyn. Don would arrive in his own truck from a job site in Surrey. Marilyn's sister stayed at the house with Jana.

"I hear my dead beat of a husband is going to be joining us," Marilyn stated half in a statement and half asking confirmation from Suzy.

"That's correct. Mr. Byers arrived home in the early hours of the morning and joined Sergeant Fitzgerald and Sergeant Chapman at the detachment shortly after arriving back in Canada."

"Just what I need, him and that mother of his telling me again what a lousy mother I am." Marilyn whined, "If he wasn't such a mamma's boy and such an old stick in the mud, he would have been here for his son. Don't know what good talkin' with him is going to be. He wasn't even around to see the kid grow up let alone know anything that would be helpful to get Tommy home." She then stared out the window in silence for the rest of the ride.

As they pulled into the reserved parking spot Suzy could see Don walking towards the entrance. "He looks like an old man." Suzy thought to herself as she put the car into park to let Marilyn out. As she opened the passenger's door for Marilyn, Suzy suspected that Marilyn had taken something to 'take the edge off' so to speak, before leaving home, for when she stepped out of the car now she seemed unsteady on her feet.

"I need to use your ladies room before I do anything more." Marilyn said to Suzy, who thought that it would be best to escort Marilyn so she did not have the opportunity to take anything more of whatever she may have in her purse.

"Put your purse here Marilyn" Suzy said, indicating the counter beside the sinks. "I'll keep an eye on it for you." then moved to wash her own hands at the sink as Marilyn headed for one of the cubicles.

Moments later realizing she had not proved much by having the purse left out of the cubicle as Marilyn had pockets in her designer, hipster jeans and matching jacket. She could have concealed a stash of her choice if she had a mind to have some on hand. Suzy observed that Marilyn always took great care that her appearance flattered her well proportioned body. High heeled-sandals, a blouse that was very low cut, short-style revealing her mid-driff as she moved her sleek body forward to wash her hands and then reaching up to assure her hair was in place. "Let's go," Marilyn said as she picked up her purse and headed for the door.

Chapter 14

Dave Byers had showered and shaved then joined Sean and Leanne for breakfast at the ABC Restaurant. Sean asked, "Do you know what you want Dave?"

"Actually I am feeling a little queasy so toast and coffee will be all I can handle. Thank you." Dave replied, "What is the plan for the meeting?"

Leanne answered, "Constable Wong is bringing Marilyn into the detachment and Don will come in from his job site. We will sit down with all of you together and go over the information, with you present so you have all the information that they have given us. If you have any questions you want to ask them you think may help clarify something we will give you the opportunity to do so. However, we would ask that you do not let personal feelings, regarding your relationships with each other or your emotional reactions addressed in this meeting."

"No worry on my part, I long ago gave up on trying to make sense out of anything Marilyn does and as far as her live-in boyfriend is concerned I feel sorry for the guy. Anyone who lives with her and her tantrums is to be pitied more than anything. It's my son I care about and I need to know everything that led up to his disappearance." Dave said, with a slight catch in voice when he talked his about his son.

The rest of breakfast went on without too much conversation, as did the short ride back to the detachment where Sean led Dave to a conference room that held a large table with seating for twelve people. "Please make yourself comfortable Dave," he said as he pulled out one of the end seats. "I am going to set up for recording our interview and we will be ready to go when Sergeant Chapman returns."

Meantime Leanne met with Constable Wong outside of one of the interrogation rooms where she had Marilyn waiting to be called into the meeting.

"I think we may have a little problem here," Suzy said to Leanne. "I think Marilyn may have self medicated as she seems to me a little less than sober."

"Great! Just what we need. Thanks Suzy for the heads up. At least we will be able to be prepared if she gets a little rangy," and with that she opened the door and said "Good Morning Marilyn."

After the pleasantries were over Leanne led Marilyn into the conference room where they joined Dave Byers, Sean, and Don Aftonson, who were sitting in silence.

You could see the looks exchanged by Marilyn and Dave as she joined them at the table. Don, just as he had in the first morning when Sean spoke with him, seemed like a beaten man. You could see he was visibly shaken and probably a little worried about Dave being present. Don slouched over the table and did not make eye contact with Marilyn as she came in.

"Don certainly looks like an abused spouse" Leanne thought to herself. "If he knows anything more than he has told us he is probably afraid to tell anyone."

Sean broke the silence by informing everyone that this interview was being taped so that there would be an accurate record of the conversations. After stating who all is present, Sean added, "We know there are some relationship difficulties between you but we are here to help find Tommy so please put those difficulties on hold during this meeting. I am going to go over with you again the events of the night before Tommy went missing and the early morning hours when you realized he was missing. Tommy's father, Dave, will be sitting in so he can be aware of all the information you have to offer. We felt that would be the best way for him to be brought up to date and for us to see if there is anything that may have been forgotten yesterday. Once we have covered all the information again I have told Dave that if he has any questions he wants to ask that he can do so at that time."

Turning to Marilyn, Sean said, "We are also going to require that you, Marilyn and you, Don talk to us alone for a few minutes after the group session." Does everyone understand the intentions here? Marilyn? "

"Yeh, yeh! But don't know how this is helpin' find Tommy! Shouldn't you be out there looking for him?" Her slur a little more obvious now.

"Oh for Christ's sake Marilyn," Don shouted and he turned his fiery eyes towards her. "Your kid is missing. Couldn't you stay sober long enough to come to a meeting to help them find him."

"Yeh, well maybe that's the only way I could get to the meeting! He's my kid. Maybe dead somewhere. What am I suppose to do while we go through these questions over and over again?" Marilyn spit back at him and started to stand up but fell back into her chair.

Excusing himself for a moment Sean called Leanne aside "Maybe you could get Constable Wong to take Marilyn back into another room and get her some coffee. She can rest there until we are finished with this meeting. She will be of no help in the state she is in anyway. We can go over the information with Don so Dave hears firsthand what they say happened. That should take a while. Then we will talk to Don and see if he is willing to take a polygraph test. Ask Suzy to keep an eye on Marilyn and see she has plenty of coffee. Maybe some sleep so she sobers up enough to question her further."

"Come with me Marilyn." Leanne gave her a hand in getting out of her chair and guided her to the door.

"That's right ... that's right both you are 'spineless.'" She glared at Don and at Dave. "Weak and spineless jellyfishes." She started to reel backwards, almost taking Leanne off balance and caught herself, staggered to the door. Once at the door Leanne ushered her into the safe care of Constable Suzy Wong who manoeuvred Marilyn to another conference room. Marilyn laid her head back in the comfortable, leather easy chair, as Suzy sat her down. All of a sudden Marilyn became quiet, closed her eyes and fell into a deep sleep.

Meanwhile Dave Byers was finding out the details of Tommy's disappearance. Sean was able to keep the meeting under control even though Dave obviously was frustrated and angered about what he was hearing.

"I am really sorry," Don said to Dave, "I'd give my anything to be able to have Tommy back. I really care about him. I should have been standing up for him and my own daughter. It's my fault! I will never forget that Dave." and with all that said, Don bent over, put his head in his hands and his body racked with sobs.

"Get me out of here," Dave said in a voice shaking with emotion. "Please! Just get me out of here."

Leanne asked Brandon to take Dave home to his mother's and to Dave said, "Try and get some rest and we will keep you abreast of what we find out. You need to be with family at this time and I am sure they need you there with them as well."

Brandon opened the door and Dave left the room walking like a man with the weight of the world on his shoulders.

Sean could feel for him. It is terrible to have someone missing and not know where they are, living or dead. "Back to what you do best Sean," he said to himself. "You can't help this man with tearing your own heart apart."

Chapter 15

Next morning at the detachment Leanne brought in a tray of devil food cupcakes with Devonshire cream filling. "My Dad sent these in for our coffee break Carrie." she said, addressing the receptionist.

"Wow! I was on a diet" Carrie commented, "Guess I'll start fresh tomorrow," she added as she followed Leanne to the lounge, coffee cup in hand. "Oh! By the way, Suzy called and said she is picking Marilyn Byers up at 7:30 a.m. for the polygraph test and she will bring you the report when it is completed. You should have the results by lunch time."

"That's great. Is Sean in yet?" Leanne turned into the lounge, seeing Sean was already there she added "Guess you don't need to answer that question." Turning towards Sean, Leanne greeted him with a smile. "Hey buddy, look what we have for coffee break!"

"Tell George he should be sainted." Sean reached for the cupcake, took a bite and looked as if he had died and gone to heaven. "Food fit for the God's." He popped the remaining morsel into his mouth and licked the last of the cream from his fingertips. "Finger lickin' good!" then reached for the tap to remove the last of the sticky residue. Drying his hands and turning to Carrie, he asked, "Carrie, could you call Suzy and Brandon and see if they can be free for two o'clock this afternoon for a meeting with Leanne and me?"

"Will do!" Carrie answered as she headed out the door "By way Sean, the media people have been phoning to talk to you. They're wondering if we have any concrete information in the Tommy Byers case and if you are planning a press conference to update them on any new developments."

"Thanks Carrie, I will call a press conference late afternoon once we have had our meeting." Then turning to Leanne, Sean asked if they could meet in his office for a little pre-meeting if she was free for a few minutes.

"No problem...see you then." Leanne replied.

Carrie called Sean saying that Brandon and Suzy are going to be tied up with Don and Marilyn so the meeting would need to be rescheduled.

"Tell them we will reschedule then and I'll text to see what works for them." Sean requested of Carrie.

***

That afternoon Sean told the press what he could but of course nothing about working with Joanna or what she was able to tell them. The evening news on all the local stations played the interview with Sean.

Chapter 16

Leanne met up with Sean just before going home for supper. "Did you hear anything back regarding the polygraph test Don took?"

"Yes. It appears even though he is really upset and appears riddled with guilt, about what has happened, his test shows no deception." Sean said, "It remains to be seen about the Marilyn, as we had to put off her test as you know. We will try to get Marilyn Byers in here sober tomorrow, but in the meantime I am going to call Joanna Lenardi to see if she has come up with any new information."

"Well, when you see her, you can tell her I found out that Dave Byers, the father, had sent Tommy a brown teddy bear for his birthday but Marilyn had sent it back to him with a note that read, "He don't need your Teddy Bears nor the goofy clothes your mom sent either! Send money!"

"You mean the boy never received the teddy bear? Yet the boy in Joanna's dream is toting one along with him? Now that is coming straight out of the Twilight Zone." exclaimed Sean. "I wonder what Joanna will have to say about that."

Sean was surprised at the excitement he was experiencing. Was it the thought of seeing Joanna again? The strange relationship to the Teddy Bear that wasn't there or a "knowing" as the new agers call it, that more would be coming through this unseen source than he might understand at the moment?

A call over the intercom paging Sean to come to the reception interrupted his thoughts and conversation with Leanne. "I'll call you later Leanne and let you know what I find out." With that he headed to the reception room where he found himself taking a deep breath and felt his heart rate accelerate. Joanna Lenardi was there waiting for him at the reception desk.

"Nice to see you again Ms. Lenardi ... Joanna," Sean gave her one of his broad, warming smiles and took her outstretched hand. "Won't you come with me to my office?" he added as he put one hand on her elbow to direct her away from the reception area.

"It is nice to see you again as well," Joanna smiled and moved along with him. "Funny how comfortable I feel in his presence" she thought as they walked along.

Sean pulled out the chair in front of his desk and when Joanna sat down he moved to the other side sitting in the comfortable desk chair, leaned back and swirling it in place to face Joanna and asked, "To what do I owe the pleasure of your company?"

Joanna replied, "This may be nothing or it may be something but in meditation this morning I saw Tommy again. Still in the same pyjamas and with the brown teddy bear."

Tommy said "Tell Daddy that I have the bear and I call him Davey after daddy. I'm not scared 'cause I have Davey Bear and a blue angel with me."

At that Sean sat straight up in his chair. "Joanna! I don't know where all this comes from. This is all new to me but I'm going to tell you what we have learned, that you have given us confirmation, with your dreams or meditations from whatever source you tap into. Once I tell you what I have I want you to explain to me, the best you can, as to how you are able to do this with such accuracy and without previously knowing any of the circumstances or the facts. This is far more than guess work, Joanna; it's beyond body language interpretation or smoke and mirror trickery."

Joanna had to giggle a little inside as she has experienced this most of her life. She said to Sean, "It really is very simple, as sometimes information comes in dreams, sometimes when awake, other times in meditation and yet other times it seemed to just come as a natural part of one's day.

Sean told Joanna about the gift of a brown teddy bear Dave Byers had sent to his son and how Marilyn had returned it and other gifts from Dave's mother with a nasty note. "Tommy never received the bear, yet you see him with it? He says it is from his Dad and he names it for his Dad." Sean leans across the desk and looks deep into Joanna's eyes as he continues. "Joanna, I am really baffled at this one."

Joanna replies, "It really is a curiosity, if he did not get the bear and his mother sent it back, as to why I see him with a Teddy Bear he did not get. Sometimes I am amazed at some of the things I encounter even though I have been working with the spiritual side of life for many years. Just like this Teddy Bear. If you are positive that Tommy did not get the present from his dad in the world here, he has it in the world of spirit. If it has not been given to him, even I am at a loss to why he totes the bear with him. I have to be true to what I receive and not withdraw or back track. This is not out of ego but out of confidence in the messages being from the highest and best of possible sources, God."

"Thank you Joanna, I would expect nothing less than the truth from you. I know you had no way of knowing about the bear so the fact that Tommy shows himself to you, in his pyjamas carrying the bear is amazing in itself. I'm sure it will have meaning to us as we unravel this mystery further," Sean said. "I have meetings for the rest of the day but if you are not busy tonight could we get together for supper about seven?"

"I would love that but I have a group meeting tonight. Maybe you would like to join me for a snack and refreshment afterwards. Say 9:30?"

"I'll be there!" Sean said with the enthusiasm of a young man getting his first invitation to accompany the prom queen to the school homecoming dance. Sean stood up and moved to the far side of the desk, took Joanna's hands in his two hands, helped her to her feet and looked deep into her velvet-brown eyes. There was a feeling that magnetic energy was drawing him ever closer to her.

Their eyes locked together in the warmth of the moment and neither of them spoke. The world around them seemed to have disappeared until Sean's phone rang and interrupted their mood.

"See you at 9:30 Sean," Joanna spoke in almost a whisper. Both she and Sean knew something had happened in that moment that would take them to a different level in their relationship if they chose to go there. Joanna wondered if that was wise to mix personal feelings into their professional relationship. This was all new to her as she had never had to worry about whether she was emotionally becoming involved with client or associates.

Her ethical line was clearly drawn so she never had been in a situation quite like this before. "I must be careful here she thought as she drove home. He is a great guy and I know he is also wrestling with his ethics and professional protocol here as well," Joanna thought to herself. "Besides the fact he has some deep emotional scars to deal with which could leave him wide open to another deep emotional incident that could be emotionally and ethically devastating to him" Out loud she said "Hey you angels, help me here to do the right thing. I am only human, you know and he is a very attractive man with a smile that could melt your angel hearts." Then laughing at herself she pulled into her driveway.

"Funny, how a perfect stranger can come into your life and change it forever." Joanna thought to herself. She already was very aware that life would not ever be the same as before Sean Fitzgerald and she crossed pathways. "Are we kindred spirits?" she queried.

Joanna readied herself for the evening ahead. There would be many who need her attention to their situations, so she could help spirit bring peace into their hearts. Her thoughts about Sean Fitzgerald needed to be put away for now.

Chapter 17

Sean and Joanna enjoyed a light meal and more interesting conversation about this world Joanna partly lived in as they relaxed in the Meditation Garden. Sean was quite at home here now.

"This is so strange to you Sean. I know, it is even harder to believe that all of us have the ability to expand our everyday natural senses; to hear more, feel more, see more, know more, and smell more than what is in our conscious world. This ability to know outside of ourselves is not for just a few chosen people, but we are now learning not all things have a logical explanation. We are all able to know things outside of our conscious reality," Joanna explains to Sean. "Many of us have to retrain ourselves to get in touch with the natural awareness we are born with and are able to use as infants and as young children. Most of us, who do not keep that ability open, shut it down as we become older and learn other methods of communication. We have to learn this intuitive skill all over again."

Joanna continued, "Then there are a few, like me, who seem to keep that awareness open a little more than the average child. Some of us, who stay aware, hone the abilities. Then some do not choose to do so and let it lie dormant. Youngsters who really keep this communication skill open seem to be those who are loners by choice or circumstance," Joanna explained.

"And were you a loner Joanna?" Sean asked as he looked into her eyes once more, feeling as if he had dove into a pool that ran deep into the core of Universal Source, a place where great secrets are revealed.

"Actually, I was left alone a lot. I was raised for many years at my Grandparents' home. They own a vineyard in Italy where they grew grapes to produce wine at the family winery. You may have heard of it Lenardi Fine Wines. The winery is world renowned. Anyway, I explored every inch of the family land as a small child. The whole family was involved in the business and my father and mother travelled to other countries as marketing representatives leaving me with my Grandparents months at a time. My parents and my grandparents loved me and gave me a wonderful life but until I left to go to boarding school in England, at eleven, I spent many hours reaching into other worlds for companionship. The angels always seemed to be with me as I roamed the hillsides and children, who had passed back into spirit, would come and play with me. I learned to talk to those in another dimension through a thought–like language. It is now just second nature to me to have spirit beings around me and communicating with me through an expanded sensory perception of all the senses God gave me. So you see, I am not much different than you are Sean, I just pay more attention to the energy activities that is around all of us."

This had answered many unanswered questions Sean had pondered about since they first met. The question of how she affords the estate she has, for one. It did not seem that she was a con, but Sean had often wondered, "Where did the money come from, to sustain such a life style?" This was a question that seemed to have haunted him. This centre alone must cost a pretty penny and it did not seem the sanctuary really brought in large amounts of money at the services and functions as everything was by donation. Many of those who came did not have much to give but their gratitude.

Knowing now, Joanna is the grand-daughter of one of the richest men in the world, Giorgio Lenardi, of Lenardi Fine Wines, gave an answer Sean was able to understand. The sincerity and honesty of Joanna's intentions can be just that. There really was no larceny in her activities and he could now let go of the negative suspicious thoughts that plagued him since they first met.

What was so surprising to Sean was how relieved he was by this information. "This isn't like me to be so personally involved with the personal life of people who will be out of my life in a week or two." Sean thought to himself. Then the thought that Joanna would be out of his life made his stomach sink. "Better watch yourself, Sean, my boy. You're walking where angels fear to tread."

As he usually did after walking back to the sanctuary with Joanna, he took a moment or two to return to his own world logic and reality before started the car and headed home

Sean came into the office early to get a head start on the paper work he needed to see to and time to review Tommy Byers' file. "Good Morning Carrie," Sean said giving her a big smile as he picked up things from his message box.

"Oh! Hi Sean," Carrie replied just a little hurried as she connected to the next call coming into the switchboard. She held up a finger to Sean so he would know she wanted to talk to him.

The call now dealt with, she turned back to Sean. "Brandon would like to talk to you and asked me to let you know as soon as you came in." Carrie added.

"Is he here now?" Sean queried and he again had to wait while Carrie answered a call.

"Sorry about the phones, there must be something in the new moon that is causing such a rush of early callers," Carrie chided. "Brandon said he will be in by 8:30 a.m. and he will see you then or if you have to leave and cannot wait, could you give him a call."

"I have lots of work to do here this morning so I will be here. Could you ask him to come by when he comes in?" Then added "What about Leanne, has she said when she will be in?"

"Like you, Leanne is an early bird this morning. I think you find he in the lounge if she is not in her office."

After dropping by his office and grabbing his coffee cup, Sean headed for the lounge. Leanne was in there with a plate of cinnamon rolls, her coffee cup freshly filled and looking over the Tommy Byers file.

"Seen anything we missed on the first go around Leanne?" Sean called over his shoulder as he poured coffee into his own cup, then he walked towards the table where Leanne was seated.

"Nothing that will give us a hot lead to Tommy's whereabouts I'm afraid," Leanne answered. "What about you, any more information from *"beyond"* that may help us?"

"Funny you should ask. Joanna saw an interesting vision where Tommy mentions the Teddy Bear he got from his father. He says he called the bear Davey Bear after his dad. You and I both heard Dave Byers say he sent a teddy bear but Marilyn Byers had sent it back to him. Now that is one for the books, the Teddy Bear who wasn't there, is there."

"This is right out of the Twilight Zone," Leanne said, "Maybe we need to talk to Dave Byers again to be sure the bear was sent back to him."

"Good idea Leanne. Can you do that sometime today? Where is he staying by the way?"

"He's at his mom and dad's place. And yes.
I will call him. I'm sure he would appreciate us just touching base with him anyway."

"Good! Now are those George's cinnamon buns?" Sean asked as he rubbed his tummy.

"You bet they are. You know my dad. He has to keep our strength up by feeding us. Help yourself, he sent them for all of us."

"Brandon is on the way in and wants to meet with me. I think he may have something new. What about Suzy? Have you heard anything new from her?" Sean queried as he put the last of the cinnamon bun into his mouth.

"She and Brandon have been checking out the guests at the party and talking to the family members. Suzy will be in at 8:30 this morning so maybe we all could get together for a quick update on what we all have learned since the last meeting."

"Great idea, maybe if you can talk to Dave Byers before we meet then we might be able to get a few more of the pieces together. Right now I feel we only have half the picture put together. Some important pieces of the puzzle are missing."

Leanne and Sean had been in this type of situation many times before. Their partnership was comfortable because they could always depend on each other to do the job to the best of their individual abilities. "This was the way partners should work," Sean thought to himself.

Chapter 19

Leanne spoke into the phone when Dave Byers answered her call. "Mr. Byers, this is Sergeant Leanne Chapmen. Could I have a minute of your time?"

"Yes, most certainly but call me Dave. Is there something new about my son?" Dave Byers said with a ring of hope in his voice.

"We felt we should touch base with you. Be assured Dave, that we are working really hard to bring Tommy home but nothing new to tell you right now." She continued, "I do have a question though. You mentioned that you sent a Teddy Bear to Tommy and Marilyn sent it back. Is that right?"

"Yes, that is correct. Marilyn sent it back to me with the note as I told you." Dave stated and added, "I sent it again with some money for her and asked if she would please let Tommy have the bear. It didn't come back so I hope she gave it to him." Dave said. "Is there something about the bear I should know about?"

"No, no." Leanne said. "Sergeant Fitzgerald just asked us to go over the conversations we have had with everyone. Often when we do that we find something that we missed the first time. Just like in this conversation. You let us know he did get the bear later. Small facts that we miss may be something or it may be nothing but we need to know all the facts to do our job."

"I understand and appreciate everything you and your other officers are doing," Dave said. "Anything I can do to help I will."

"Thank you Dave, we will keep you posted on what we know. In the meantime, know many people are praying for Tommy and your family."

Leanne prepared the rest of her report for the meeting and a few minutes later she was joined by Sean, Brandon and Suzy.

Everyone took a place around the table with beverage cups and the remaining cinnamon rolls Leanne brought in.

Sean turned to Brandon and asked him to share what he has found in the investigation with the guests attending the party the night before Tommy was reported missing.

"Suzy and I have talk to the guests," Brandon stated. "We also talked to some of the family members who were at the party. While I spoke to Marilyn's sister she told me about a man she believed was a sailor from a ship that was in harbour that day. He had been invited to the party by a male friend of hers. She gave me the name and contact number for her friend. I questioned this friend and he says he met this guy in a bar in Vancouver and invited him to come to the party. He said the fellow had a hard to pronounce name but he said he can't remember the name as the sailor said to call him Rev. He believes Rev was part of the sailor's last name. He does not know the name of the ship but he is pretty sure the sailor said it was a Polish ship."

"Did you get a description of what he looked like?" Sean asked.

"Yes, they gave a description of a man who was dressed in dark clothing with a navy pea jacket. He wore a toque rolled up, had thick curly black hair, burly build about 5' 10" tall. He had a duffle bag with him, as they remember." Brandon added, "Both the sister and her friend remember he said his ship was leaving Vancouver at 5 a.m. so we might be able to check what ships sailed that morning at that time."

"Good job you two. Yes, follow up on the ships that were due to leave at 5 a.m. That will be a great place to start to see if this guy knows something about Tommy's disappearance."

Sean could all but contain himself about this unknown guest. The description certainly matched the vision that Joanna had about the man on the gangplank with the duffle bag slung over his shoulder. It would explain why he seemed to be looking around as he ran up the gangplank if he is involved in some way.

"Okay, Leanne what about the phone call with Dave Byers? Do you have anything new to report from Dave?" Sean shifted his attention to Leanne.

"Well it appears that Marilyn sent the Teddy Bear back with the note Dave told us about but later he sent the bear back with some money for her. He asked her to let the boy have the Teddy Bear. It appears that she may have let the boy have the bear from his father once he sent her the money." Leanne answered as she shook her head from side to side in almost disbelief of how a mother could be so cold and heartless.

Leanne thought to herself, "She has to be the coldest woman I ever met. What did she have kids for anyway? She is so self absorbed. Everything is about her."

Meanwhile, Sean was secretly excited inside as he now could put some of Joanna's psychic vision pieces into the puzzle. The Teddy Bear that wasn't there ... was there. The man, fitting the description of the sailor at the party running up the gangplank of a ship, looking around like he is being pursued in the dark of the night, the missing wet pajamas and the vision of Tommy that Joanna first came to talk to him about, all too close to what they are finding to be the actual events. Sean did not know anyone who could just guess the facts in a case with such accuracy.

He not only has a need to find Tommy but to look further into this ability Joanna possesses and to find out how it is possible to know what she knows from a source outside of the world Sean lives in. Even to the Duffle bag. "Did this duffle bag hold a clue to Tommy's whereabouts? Could he be in the duffle bag?"

"Thanks everyone." Sean said relating the next plan of action each of them would follow. "Brandon, you and Suzy follow up on the sailor and the ships departing from the Port Metro Vancouver around 5 a.m. the day Tommy went missing. Leanne and I will talk to the mother and stepfather again to see if we can get any information on this guy. As soon as you have anything to report call me. It is important to keep close contact on this so if we need to move quickly that we are all aware of what is needed."

Suzy and Brandon nodded in agreement. "We'll let you know what we find out as soon as we can." Suzy said "Have a great day." And with that the two young constables left the room.

Leanne too got up to leave when Sean asked her to stay a few minutes longer as he wanted to share what Joanna had seen in her vision of the man on the gangplank of a ship.

Sean pulled out all of the taped recordings he had of Joanna's visions during their meetings starting with the first time Joanna had come to the office and asked about the wet pajamas and asked Leanne to listen to each of them.

When they had listened to all of the recordings Leanne said, "Sean that is amazing. Surely you have to believe there is something in this psychic stuff now. There is information there that we did not know before today and we know she did not get that information out of guess work. No one could just randomly guess facts that are that accurate. Are you going to call her and tell her where we are in the investigation and see if she can help put the pieces together?"

"I thought the same thing, Leanne. I don't know if she can link the psychic dots, so to speak. I think she may be able to get additional information to help us see more of what went on in that house the night of the party and who knows something they are not telling us about. She may be able to see where Tommy is and most importantly, if he is still alive."

"Sean, I would love to go with you but truthfully you are working well with Joanna on your own. I think at this point of the game, you need to continue just as you are." Leanne replied, "but I am taking a rain check on the offer to go and watch her work at her centre one night. You really did not say too much about what happened at the demonstration night you attended."

"Well, I will tell you this much, it was very interesting and appeared to be very accurate according to those who were recipients of messages. We will need to go out one night for supper while I tell you all about it. Better yet, we'll have supper and attend an evening at the centre. I always wanted to know your deepest secrets," Sean teased.

"And I want to know all about you as well," Leanne teased right back. "Especially about this glint you get in your eye when you mention Joanna's name. Something I should know about Sean?"

Sean thought he was keeping his feelings about Joanne inside where no one could see but obviously his long partner-relationship with Leanne had given her an insight into his inner most feelings. Leanne was so much a loving, motherly type of person it was hard to keep much from her maternal instinct.

Leanne got up to leave and Sean realized what a fortunate person he was to have Leanne as a partner. She may like to tease him from time to time but he knew Leanne was a true and loyal friend as well as the best partner anyone could have.

As Leanne had her hand on the door knob she heard Sean say, "Thanks Leanne," causing Leanne to turn and face him. There was an unspoken moment where both partners just felt that bond that goes a step beyond friend or co-worker to link kindred spirits. Leanne knew he had been there for her in tough times and Sean never doubted she would be there for him for whatever he needed.

"You're welcome, my friend." That said, Leanne left Sean to his own resources.

Chapter 21

The phone in Joanna's office rang and as was her normal manner, she answered with a wonderful uplifting tone to her voice. "Haven of Prosperity, Joanna speaking."

"Sean here Joanna. Is it possible to get a few minutes with you this afternoon?"

"I am free until 3 p.m. today, Sean." Joanna then added, "Why not join me for lunch at noon."

"Great. Let me bring dessert. See you then." Sean hung up the phone and paused for a moment to enjoying the essence of Joanna ... that he felt just talking to her. He was beginning to realize the whole world did seem just a little brighter and his step a little lighter after talking to Joanna.

Sean dropped back to his home to freshen up before going to the centre. Then dropped by his favorite bakery, he picked some chocolate éclairs and cream puffs to take for dessert.

Sean pulled into the parking spot closest to the residential entrance and went to the door to ring the bell.

Joanna answered the door. She wore white calf length Capri's, white sandals, with a small elevated heel, showing off her shapely legs, and a white drawstring blouse that revealed her smooth copper tone shoulders. Her ravenous hair, sides drawn into a clipped in the back, let her hair careen almost to her waist in light, natural curls Sean was overwhelmed by her natural beauty as she wore very little make-up. He felt a catch in his throat as she reached for his hand and brought him into the foyer of the residence.

"Come with me," Joanna said as she led Sean to the patio off the dining room. The French doors opened into yet another garden of flowers, shrubs and manicured grass. Bird baths and fountains as well as flagstone pathways allowed one to relax in nature.

Comfortable patio furniture would let them dine in comfort.

"This is for dessert," Sean said, offering the bakery boxes to Joanna.

"Thank you. I bet they are almost sinful. I have a real sweet tooth you know." She placed them on the side table she realized Sean was still standing.

"Have a seat Sean. There is ice tea in the pitcher or if you prefer I can get you a coffee," Joanne stated.

"Ice tea is great," Sean said taking one of the comfortable chairs. To himself he said, "She is really breathtakingly beautiful."

Joanna poured tea for Sean and she poured one for herself. "I thought we would eat first and then stroll in the garden while we talk. Is that okay with you?"

"I'm in your hands," Sean chided, as he leaned back throwing his arms wide open. A silent thought ran through his mind, "I really am in her hands. Right now I could not say no if my life depended on it."

Joanna reached into the under counter fridge and brought out a plate of sandwiches and placed them on the table. A variety of pickles, olives, cheeses and other condiments were also brought from the fridge. The soup tureen held Cream of Potato soup that was ambrosia for the Gods. Potato soup was one of Sean's favourites but he had to admit this was the best he had ever eaten.

They made small talk as the ate, enjoying the sounds of nature and the closeness of each other but Sean would have been hard pressed to say what they talked about. He felt as if he were in a wonderful dream world which he hoped he would never need to leave.

The dessert was delicious and they both decided to share their choice of pastries with the other so they both could savour it all. As they leaned over tasting each other's delicate treats, it seemed so intimate and pleasurable that they almost lost track of time.

Joanna was the first to break the spell as she realized how long they had sat and enjoyed the lunch and each other's company.

"Come with me Sean. Let me show you my inner garden as we talk about why you called."

Walking through the garden Sean filled Joanna in on the new events. About the bear that really was there, about the sailor with the duffle bag being at the party and how accurate she was about everything she had given them from the wet pajamas to the description of the sailor with the duffle bag.

"Do you think that now we have validated your information that you will be able to connect those psychic dots and possibly lead us to where he is?" Sean asked Joanne.

"Yes, I think if we can take a couple of hours and just go from the boy missing from the home to each event as we know it then the other pieces may fall into place. We may get more information or get more out of what we already have." Joanna added, "I do have an appointment this afternoon, can you possibly come tonight Sean? We will go to the Meditation Garden and we can give uninterrupted attention to the information."

"Yes. Is 9:30 okay with you?" Sean asked. "I will bring all the information that we have and all the information that you have given us so we can hopefully combine your psychic talents and my profiling techniques to find Tommy."

"I hope and pray that we can find Tommy and bring him home," Joanna said in an almost a prayer like tone."

As Joanna walked Sean to the door she turned to him, holding both his hands in hers, "Until tonight. Angels go with you, my friend."

Sean could hardly remember walking to his car. He sat for five minutes to just let himself settle back into the everyday-work-a-day world.

Driving his car out onto the street Sean thought to himself about his life with another wonderful lady who had stolen his heart.

"I swore I would never totally give my heart to anyone again," Sean said to himself as the negative side of him brought out all the cynical thinking. "Love just hurts too damn much."

Yet here he was, opening his heart up to risk life's cruel twists shattering it once more. Or was Joanna the one that was to help him heal from that horrific pain? Was she the one that would make his life have meaning once more beyond his work? Was she the one who would prove to him that new love can and will heal the aching heart?

Leanne had been telling him for year, "You're a great guy Sean. You're a good friend and a trusted partner but you pull back when it comes to commitments of the heart. One day you will fall in love with the right woman and be able to open up completely to her. One day you will find a passionate reason for living and realize that you honour those you love best by living well and being all you can be. To do that Sean you will need to take a chance on love and gamble it all."

Leanne had experienced a lot of pain in her life too. When she lost her husband she seemed to pick up the pieces and go on. Sean did not know how she was able to stay so positive. Was it for her boys and her Dad?

Certainly she had a different way of dealing with the pain. There was no doubt that there was great love in their marriage or that she cried many nights into her pillow but somehow Leanne went on to have a fulfilled life.

"I'm going to try to take a page out of Leanne's book and accept the wonderful experience of having Joanna in my life for whatever that will be." As he thought about Joanna the memory of the wonderful time he had just spent with her pushed away any negative thoughts and the warm feelings crept into his consciousness.

As he stepped out of his car, he could see Leanne coming towards him.

"Hi there, Sean. Just what have you been up to?" Leanne teased. "You look like the cat that swallowed the canary. If I was asked to guess what was going on, I'd say you're a man in love."

"Well that's for me to know and for you to find out, Miss Snoopy." Laughing as he entered the building.

"I'll be back in a short while. Please wait for me." Leanne called after him as she stepped into her own car.

"Will do. Have some things to do here before I leave." Sean then opened the door and went to reception.

"Hi Carrie." Sean gave her his usual warm smile and started to pick up his messages.

"Hi Sean, Leanne said she would be back in as soon as she could. She said she needed to look into something and asked if you to wait for her if you could."

"Yes, thank you Carrie. I saw her outside when I came in. Have her come to my office when she returns." Sean headed for his office whistling, "Love Makes the World Go Round." He almost danced his way back to his office as he read his messages.

Carrie, who had felt all along, behind all those warm smiles and twinkling eyes, there was something missing in Sean's life. She also realized something was different about him today. "Things that make you go Hmm?" she thought to herself. The switchboard lit up again and Carrie was back to business and had little time to ponder the mental questions she had about Sean's unusual behaviour.

Chapter 22

Leanne met up with Constable Suzy Wong and Constable Brandon Ellis in the cafeteria at The Port of Metro Vancouver. They had been investigating the possibility of an unknown person of interest that was possibly a sailor off a ship leaving at 5 a.m. the morning Tommy went missing.

Brandon started the conversation. "There was a Polish ship that left at 5 a.m. on the day Tommy disappeared and there was a deck hand named Solotoff Revenoffolis aboard that ship. That would fit with the Rev name. We were able to get a picture of him from his ID card on file."

Suzy added, "And we have information that that same ship will be coming into port the day after tomorrow. We may be able to question him then."

"We asked the port manager if there is any way to find if he is still aboard that ship." Brandon stated and then added, "The port manager contacted the captain in confidence and asked if this deckhand is still aboard and the captain said he is."

"Good work you two," Leanne complimented her two constables and asked them to get all the details together concerning time the ship would be docking and arrange to have the deckhand brought to the detachment so she and Sean may talk to him first hand.

"In the meantime you two get all the information you can on the deckhand, his past history, etc. We may be dealing with someone who is more directly involved in this than we know. We cannot take a chance that if he is our person responsible for Tommy's disappearance and he gets wind of us waiting for him, and takes flight. Also can you get back and talk to Sean as soon as possible. He may have further instructions for you." Leanne stood up and prepared to leave and once again said, "Good job. Well done you two."

Leanne headed back to the detachment to meet with Sean to keep him up–to–date with the latest on the deckhand. "Another hit for Joanna," she thought to herself. "More pieces to the puzzle, not long now 'til we break this case. I can feel it in my bones."

Chapter 23

Leanne parked in her spot at the detachment and quickly moved toward the entrance doors. As she passed Carrie she mouthed the words, "Is Sean in his office?" and Carrie nodded all the while dealing with someone who needed directions on where they were located.

Seeing Sean was alone in his office Leanne made a light knock and went in. "Think we may have a break in the case coming very soon Sean," Leanne stated. "We think we have found the seaman we were looking for from the night of the party."

"Really? Good job Leanne." He rose to his feet to give her a 'hi five'.

"Well in fact it was Suzy and Brandon who tracked him down," Leanne said. "The captain of his ship is aware we need him for an inquiry and will keep the fact of that from him until the ship docks and we can pick him up for questioning."

"Brandon and Suzy are getting all the details on Rev's history as well as the ETA of the ship. They will share all that with you when they come in. You should have that information before you meet with Joanna tonight. She may be able to give us more insight so we have more to work with when we question this guy. His full name is Solotoff Revenoffolis."

"That would account for the name 'Rev' wouldn't it!" Sean replied. "His name is rather unusual for most people to remember."

"Want to get a bite to eat before Suzy and Brandon get here?" Leanne asked Sean. "I haven't eaten since the muffins Dad sent in for our coffee break this morning."

"I'm good, had a fantastic lunch." Sean's thoughts drifted back to the wonderful companion that made the luncheon one to remember. He must have got that glassed over look on his face again. It was a dead give away to Leanne.

"I assume the company wasn't half bad either?" Leanne chided and then added, "Are you having supper tonight too then?"

"Tonight is strictly business Leanne," Sean said half trying to convince himself that it was just business with a very lovely lady.

"Sure Sean, I believe you, thousands wouldn't but I do." And with that she giggled and left to pick up a sandwich at the ABC Restaurant.

After Leanne left, Sean recaptured the beautiful essence of his lunch with Joanna. He knew this was not the time for a full blown romance between them and also remembered he must deal with his past before he dare take on another person into a significant relationship. It could break his heart but more importantly it would not be fair to any woman to have her give him her heart when he could only give part of himself into any relationship. He would always be waiting for 'the other shoe to drop' as the saying goes for every time a little happiness came his way it was snatched away by some cruel twist of fate.

First the loss of his wonderfully, charismatic father, the loss of his mother through all those years of her addiction and low self esteem and her death, then there was Marlene, his beautiful bride of ten months.

How does one get over the death of a person you love more than life itself and that sweet baby girl that died two hours after her mother.

Marlene's kidney failure had also affected the baby and the doctors could do nothing more. Everyone said it was not his fault but somehow it felt like it was. It seemed he had brought this unlucky energy into Marlene's life by just loving her. Everything he loved seemed to be taken away from him for some reason he did not understand.

How does one forget a beautiful, young eighteen year old girl with her baby in her arms, looking so perfect, like they were asleep in the white casket? How does a nineteen year old boy forget such a heart break and added to all the other emotional situations in his young life, trust that anything he loves will not somehow be snatched away as it has been in the past? Dare he invest again? Dare he invest again in the gamble of love and life?

"This is ecstasy and pain, to love so deeply filled with such ecstasy and then the pain of grief that never seems to end. Will Joanna be the one who may lead me out of this ring of fire, where my emotions live?" Sean thought to himself. "I don't think I could invest all of those emotions in another relationship and be able to survive abandonment again."

Oh, he knew in his head Marlene had not abandoned him on purpose any more than his father had. He knew that in his head, but emotionally, it still felt like abandonment in the very depth of his being.

How many times had friends invited out to meet some nice lady friend, but Sean had given up on ever finding someone like Marlene again before Joanna came into his life. He found himself thinking about Joanna and more than once wondered what kind of a wife she would be.

This was all new to Sean and to tell the truth it scared him more than he wanted to admit even to himself. He justified his present life by thinking, "At least, as a single guy, I am able to keep my emotions under control. I'm able to do my job I love." And as if trying to convince himself, this was the life for him said, "I am respected and am trusted with the lives of others every day so why should I want to put myself into a situation again where my emotions take me back down that black rabbit hole again. Logic should tell me that a relationship between Joanna's world and mine would never work. Our worlds are so far apart." Sean resolved to himself that he would get this fantasy world he had been living in out of his head for good, once this case was over.

Besides having emotions himself, he had no reason to think that Joanna thought of him in the same way he'd been thinking about her. Sure, she had been more than friendly towards him, but from what he had learned about her, she was a spiritually generous person with everyone.

His first impression that she must be in it for the big bucks soon proved to be a wrong conclusion, on his part. The centre took a collection at its services but it certainly was not 'big bucks' when you looked at the upkeep of the estate the centre was on. Of course Joanna received no payment for the hours she put into helping find Tommy. This was all just from the goodness of her heart. She didn't want any publicity either so there was really nothing in it for her personally.

"One thing for sure Sean Ol' boy," he said to himself, "you have to admit this has been an exciting few days and the case should be coming to a close soon. We found out who 'Rev.' is. If we are lucky we will know what happened to Tommy soon."

Chapter 24

Suzy and Brandon came to speak to Sean at his office at 4:30 p.m. and told him that the ETA for the Ship was 11:50 p.m. 'Rev' lives in a month by month hotel room in downtown Vancouver.

"We got a search warrant for his room," Brandon said, "and found nothing that indicates young Tommy has ever been there. The room, although not very fancy, was clean and other than the normal personal items one would expect to find. There was nothing suspicious."

Brandon continued on, "We talked to the desk clerk who seems to know 'Rev' quite well and he has never seen him with a young boy in the five years Rev has lived there. We talked to all the other desk clerks and employees as well. They say he is a quiet loner. They know he has a sister in Burnaby somewhere but none of them could tell us her name or where she lives."

Suzy added, "The staff at the hotel did say, however, that the last time he was in port he had met up with a couple of ladies in the bar. They drank together for a while and then he left with them between 5 and 6 p.m. Rev had his duffle bag with him so the staff who saw him assume he went straight to his ship after leaving his companions."

Suzy added, "'Rev' would often take his gear out with him on a day he had to get back to the ship. The staff said they had no reason to think anything was out of the ordinary that last day. That was the day of the house party, so I think it was Marilyn and her sister in the bar drinking with him."

"Sounds like it," Sean said "and the party went on at Marilyn's home later. We really need to talk to him. So as soon as you are able to detain him call me. I'll meet you here."

"Will do, Sean. We are going to get a bite to eat and be back shortly."

"I will go and do what I have to do. Call me as soon as you know the ship has docked. Leanne is getting a sandwich so when you see her let her know what we are doing. She will definitely want to be in on the end of this," Sean said. He felt that old familiar feeling that he always had when a case was wrapping up and everything was in place. Sean gathered his things together and prepared to leave.

At that moment Leanne walked in and joined them. "Suzy and Brandon will get you up to speed on what we have found out so if you don't mind I will go to my meeting and see you three here later."

Leanne gave Sean a smile and a wink that was missed by Suzy and Brandon. Sean left without saying anything more.

Chapter 25

Sean pulled into the parking space at the Sanctuary parking lot. As he stepped out of his car he saw Joanna talking to an older lady. It was easy to see that this older woman had found some comfort from her meeting with Joanna as she hugged her in a long embrace. Dried her eyes with her handkerchief and almost bowing to Joanna repeated "God bless you Joanna ... God bless you." Joanna embraced the older woman once more. Two younger women then took the older woman to a car in the parking lot and prepared to leave.

Joanna then saw Sean and her smile light up her whole face. Sean's heart melted once more and his resolve of earlier today almost gone out the window.

"Hi Sean, be with you in ten minutes," Joanna called out to him. "You may go to the meditation garden and meet me there if you like or wait for me here and I'll walk over with you."

"Meet you in the Meditation Garden," Sean called back to her. Thinking to himself, "I could do with a bit of quiet time on my own."

Sean had been here a few times before but not on his own, as he entered into the room where he first sat with Joanna he could feel her presence everywhere even though she was not there yet. Sean took a lounge chair and as he did he felt all the tensions of the day start to leave his body. He leaned his head on the cushioned head rest and closed his eyes for a moment.

It seemed like a dream but suddenly he was in a place outside of his world of reality. He felt himself contained inside of a warm cocoon like essence that was so peaceful. He could see a field of the greenest grass he had ever seen and hills that reminded him of the Sound of Music. He could see Marlene. His beautiful young wife holding the hand of a ten year old girl. Both Marlene and the beautiful little girl were dancing barefoot. They had chiffon dresses and chain of flowers around their heads. They danced and laughed together and it made Sean feel totally at peace to be part of this dream, if it were a dream.

Marlene came closer and spoke to Sean, "Your daughter Erin and I are always with you. We have danced for you many times so that you could see we will never leave you. We are happy my love. Danny Boy and Mary Rose are here with us. We want you to be happy Sean, to love again." With that, Sean felt her kiss his cheek and his daughter Erin jumped into his arms and kissed his cheek. She then took her mother's hand and as they floated away into the ethers of spirit, they waved and said "We love you ... live well and honour us."

At the very moment those words had been spoken Sean felt a soft touch and on his hand and a voice whisper "Sean, are you back with me?"

Sean opened his eyes to see the face of Joanna and felt the warmth of her touch on his hand.

Strange as it would seem, Sean did not feel unnerved or uneasy after this experience but a feeling of peacefulness he had not known since his father passed away.

Joanna poured a nice cup of ice tea for each of them and just let Sean return to his everyday-work-a-day world slowly. She never asked him about what happened but let him regain his composure.

In about fifteen minutes Sean seemed to be in his total awareness once more and Joanna asked if they were going to work on the case tonight.

Sean said he felt if she could get anything more that may give them any more pieces to this puzzle he would most appreciate it.

Joanna settled into a comfortable position to let herself expand her senses to connect to the higher power.

"I see an older woman, sixtyish, standing in her kitchen making soup for lunch on a tray. She takes that tray into a room where a young boy is in bed under handmade comforters. His head is bandaged and he is weak and very pale. It seems he has had a head injury and she has been nursing him. She props him up with three huge pillows and spoon feeds him the soup. She is singing songs to him in a different language than English and even though the child's language is not the one she speaks he gets comfort from her loving care and her gentle voice.

I think this is Tommy Byers. I do not feel this woman speaks much English. So I am not sure it is in Canada but yet I do not feel he was transported a long distance. So maybe just the woman is from some other country.

If it is Tommy, the reason I was able to pick his spirit up for communication is he was in a comma for a number of days. He would, therefore, leave his body and be able to communicate as any other spirit who is departed can. I feel he was left for dead somewhere. Somehow by some miracle this woman has nursed him back to health. He is not 100% yet and may need more time to heal."

At hearing this Sean is elated. Dare they hope that Tommy is alive? "Do you really think he is alive?" he asked Joanna.

"Yes, I think he is alive. Now to find him." Joanna had tears brimming at the edge of her eyes.

Sean might have kissed her at that moment but his phone sounded and he knew they would need him back at the detachment. "Sean Fitzgerald here," he answered and Leanne's voice came in excitedly that they had picked up Solotoff Revenoffolis. They were taking him to the detachment now. "I'm on my way. Thanks Leanne."

Sean turned back to Joanna and thanked her for all she had done to help them and for the great support she had given him. "I will let you know as soon as we have the boy back safe and sound."

"Please Sean. No matter what time it is, please, phone me. I will wait up for your call. Come now, we have to get you back to your car."

They move very quickly along the pathway back to the sanctuary in silence. Sean got into his car and headed into the detachment. Joanna could only wave and put up a prayer as he drove away.

"Please God, let Tommy still be alive and bring him safely home." She did not tell Sean but she may have been picking up an earlier scene. It could be Tommy was in the home of this lady who was nursing him back to health at one point. There was no guarantee that he made it and did not succumb to his injuries.

Joanna went into the her residence. Prepared her large soaker tub with lavender bath oil and lit the candles that surrounded the tub. The one way glass that allowed her to sit in the tub and view the gardens, the starlight in the sky, while enjoying the relaxing scent of lavender. Joanna was at peace with her spirit. She would stay in the warm swirling waters until her spirit felt replenished and then wrapping herself in the soft terry towel bathrobe, sit in front of the fireplace, sip chamomile tea, and listen to Revelle's Bolero on the surround sound in her bedroom. Time would not matter for it truly does not exist in the spirit realm she was visiting to refresh her body, mind and spirit.

Chapter 26

Sean arrived at the Newton RCMP Detachment and saw Leanne's car in her parking spot. Brandon and Suzy would also be there. As he came in the reception area he received a smile from the evening receptionist Louisa. "Sergeant Fitzgerald they are waiting for you in the lounge."

"Thank you Louisa." Sean said as he breezed by the reception desk.

As Sean entered the lounge Leanne said "Hi Sean...glad you are here. We have put Solotoff Revenoffolis in the interrogation room. We did not want to say too much to him until you got here."

"What have you told him?" Sean asked Leanne. "Did he know why you were bringing him here or did he volunteer any information?"

"We just told him we wanted to know about two women he met in the bar at his hotel on his last trip in port. When we mentioned these two ladies he got a little rattled and said he didn't remember being with any ladies. My gut tells me something else Sean. I think he knows a lot about that night." Leanne went on, "I think he knows what happened to the boy."

"Well let's go and meet 'Rev' and see what he has to say." With that he opens the lounge door and motions Leanne to come with him. "I want Suzy and Brandon in the observation room while you and I go in to talk to him."

Suzy and Brandon got comfortable in the observation room and Leanne and Sean entered into the interrogation room to talk to 'Rev'.

"Mr. Revenoffolis, I'm Sergeant Fitzgerald and this is my partner Sergeant Leanne Chapman, may we call you 'Rev?'"

"Sure! I have no problem with that. I thought about changing my name when I was nineteen but my dad would have been upset. It was his father's name. So Rev. is good with me." he replied. "What is this all about?"

"We want to know about the two women that you were with on your last night of your shore leave the last time you were in port. And please don't say you were not with them for we have witnesses who saw you in the bar together," Sean said directly looking him in the eye.

"Okay! I was with these two women. Had a pretty good time drinking and laughing it up," 'Rev' confessed.

"We understand that you went to a house party with them afterwards, correct?"

'Rev' looked white as a sheet and beads of sweat came out on his forehead. "Guess I better tell you the whole story. Hope I'm not going to go to jail for this. I didn't do anything except try to help the kid."

"What do you mean 'Help the kid?'" Sean asked.

"The party was going in full swing when the father of the baby came home. He was not impressed that the kids were running around in the midst of the party unfed and not in bed. He and the one named Marilyn had a dragged out screaming match and she told him to look after the kids himself, if he didn't like it leave!" 'Rev' told Sean. "Then he fed and put them in pajamas, tucked them in and started to party along with us."

"Somewhere about 2 a.m. one of the male guests was all over Marilyn and her boyfriend got pretty angry. He told the guy to get out and the guy wouldn't leave so the boyfriend took a swing at him and the other guy pounded him quite good. Tommy the kid came out screaming 'Don't hit Daddy Don...Don't hit Daddy Don' and next thing Marilyn had picked the kid up and threw him in his bed. He really bumped his head and passed out. They thought he was dead." added Rev.

"Then what happened? Did anyone call for help?" Leanne asked.

"No" Rev said, "The party broke up fast after that. The big guy who beat Don up, helped Marilyn. They wrapped Tommy up in his quilt and at that point I got out of there. I figured they killed the kid". Rev. carries on, "I didn't know what they might do next. Outside in the cold air, my mind cleared and I thought 'I have to do something' but I didn't know what. I was standing in the shadow of a tree when they came out and threw Tommy now in a plastic bag on the deck of the yellow pick up. While they stood talking I got into the back of the pickup with my duffle bag and the body of the boy and waited for them to quit talking about how they were going to get rid of the body. I lay flat on the truck bed until they pulled up to a dumpster in an industrial complex. When they got out and opened up the dumpster to see if there was room for the body I hopped out and hid with my duffle bag in the shadows of the building."

Rev. took a deep breath and continued. "After they left I dug through the dumpster to check if the kid was really dead. If so I would just leave 'cause I could do nothing for him. When I checked I heard him make a whimpering noise. I fished him out and then thought, what am I going to do now? I thought, I'll take him to my Ma who lives at my sister's house in the basement suite. Ma would know what to do."

"I knew my sister and husband were away for two months so they wouldn't know. Ma doesn't speak much english so she doesn't watch much TV news. I threw the clothes out of my duffle bag into the dumpster, tucked the kid into my duffle bag and called a cab. Ma has been looking after him ever since."

"Why didn't you call the police?" Sean shouted.

"Partly 'cause I was stupid drunk and partly 'cause if I missed my ship I'd be fired." Rev replied.

"I took him to Ma, helped her clean him up and had to leave to get back to my ship. Then when I heard the news the next day, I didn't dare call anybody 'cause they thought the kid had been nabbed and I did not want to get blamed for that. I really did not know what to do." Rev now obviously letting the whole story just pour out of him.

"Is Tommy still with your mother?" Sean said trying to keep a professional demeanor not wanting to push Rev too hard in case he decided to quit talking freely.

"Yes. With Ma, at my sister's house in Burnaby. Ma has looked after him real good. She says he is eating good now too and talks to his teddy bear that we found wrapped up with him in the quilt," Rev informed them. "The bear and very wet PJ's is all the kid had of his own when we unwrapped him from the quilt. So Ma washed him down and wrapped him in a flannel sheet 'til his PJ's were washed. Ma said he never let go of his bear except to get washed and dressed. He holds it all the time."

"Okay now, Rev. we need to know your sister's address. We will need you to call your mother and let her know we will be coming for the boy so we don't upset her. We will need you to come with us so she will not cause any fuss when we pick him up. Are you willing to do that?" Sean asked and turning to Leanne asked her to get in touch with Irene Vass, the social worker assigned to Tommy's case. "We will need to have her make the arrangements to have an ambulance at the home and she should also meet us there to take charge of the boy."

"Suzy is to pick up Dave Byers and arrange to have him meet us at the house. I want someone the boy knows and loves to be there when we have him taken to hospital. He has had more than his share of trauma. Even though, Irene will need to have him taken to the hospital, she will let Dave ride with him."

"Brandon is to escort Marilyn and Don to the hospital. He is to have a couple of other constables assist him as we need to keep tabs on those two until our investigation into what all went on in that home that night and we see what charges, if any, are to be laid."

"You and I will escort Rev. to talk to the Mrs. Revenoffolis because you understand the sensitive nature of this interview and we do not want to frighten a lady who just tried to help and has done a good job of taking care of the boy." Sean instructed then added, "Let's see if we can co-ordinate meeting Irene at the house in an hour. That gives us time to have Rev. prepare his mother and for us to get all the other things in place."

"That sounds about right Sean and I will let you know when everyone is in place and ready to go." Leanne said as she headed for the door.

Now alone Sean took advantage to make a call to Joanna, who answered on the first ring. Sean told her "The boy is alive and with a woman who has been caring for him in her daughter's Burnaby home. You were right on again, she does not speak english as a first language and not very fluent in it. I can't tell you much more now. We are on our way to get him now. I will not be able to call again until tomorrow so have a good sleep and pleasant dreams. I'll call you as soon as I can."

Chapter 27

At 11:30 p.m., Leanne came in and told Sean "Everything is ready to go and Rev's mother is quite nervous about what is happening. He told her he would come with us and not to worry. The police will be there and won't do any bad things to her. They just want to get the boy back to his family."

Leanne and Sean pulled up to the older home on Portland Street. They walked up the wooden stairs to the front porch with Rev. A small older lady met them at the door and started to talk very excitedly to her son.

Rev answered her, wrapping his arm around her shoulder and taking her hand with his other hand leading her back into the kitchen of the home. He sat her down at the table, holding her hands and explained to her what the police and others would be doing. And her soft blue eyes filled up with tears as she began to understand the boy would be leaving. She had learned to love having him there. Who would not love such a sweet child as Tommy.

Irene Vass, who was now on the scene, asked Sean if they could take the boy now. The ambulance was outside and Suzy had the boy's father Dave Byers with her in her car.

"I think we need to have Dave Byers come in in-case he wakes up as we are taking him out of the home so he does not become frightened."

Suzy brought Dave Byers in and Sean said, "We are going to take your son to BC Children's Hospital in Vancouver. We would like you to be the one to pick him up and carry him out to the ambulance and you can ride with him to the hospital. He is less apt to be frightened if you are holding him."

"Of course, thank you! Thank you!" was all Dave could say as his throat choked up and tears began to run stream down his cheeks. Then he had his sleeping son placed in his arms, wrapped in his quilt and holding his Teddy Bear close to his heart. Tommy was the picture of an angel at rest.

Opening his sleepy eyes just for a moment Tommy said, "Daddy, I knew you would come. Davey Bear and I sent you messages every day when we said our prayers." Closing his eyes he snuggled in closer to his father's chest and fell back to sleep.

Before they left, Rev's mother came over to kiss the boy's cheek and say her good-byes. She gave him a blessing in her own language and as she did so Dave Byers thanked her for looking after his boy. "We will come and see you soon. Tommy will not forget you." With that Dave left with Irene Vass.

The older woman put her head on the table and wept.

Chapter 28

Now 1:30 a.m., Leanne and Sean arrive at the hospital. Dave Byers had stayed with his son while the doctors had checked him over.

Marilyn had been creating a fuss because she was not allowed to see the boy. She had back talked the hospital staff and made a general nuisance of herself. As usual she had had more than one or two drinks.

The hospital staff isolated Marilyn and Don in a grief room and Don had said very little, hunched over with his head in his hands.

Brandon and the other constables stood by and waited and watched the antics as Marilyn got more and more verbally abusive with everyone.

Suddenly Don's head snapped up. He rose to his feet and with both hands gripped Marilyn's shoulders, planted her in the nearest chair, put his face right in hers and yelled, "Do yourself a favour and shut your mouth!" Then he sat back down head in hands.

This was so out of character for him and happened so fast that the officers had no time to react and certainly froze Marilyn in time. Her jaw dropped open and her eyes bugged out and then she closed her mouth and sat without another word until Sean and Leanne came in to talk to her an hour later.

When Leanne and Sean came in to talk to Marilyn and Don, they told them they could come and see Tommy through the glass outside of his room, before being taken to the detachment for questioning.

As they looked through the window some of the old Marilyn was returning, especially, when she saw Dave Byers in the room with her son.

Sean told her, "If you cause a ruckus we will just transport you now. If you want to see that your boy is okay and be able to go in, under supervision, to see him, you will choose to be civil."

Leanne took Marilyn in and as soon as Tommy saw her he said hysterically, "Go away! Go away!" So Leanne took her out.

Don asked if he could see the boy and Sean took him in to see him. "Daddy Don, are you alright? That bad man was hitting you and I was scared."

"I'm okay Buddy, I'm okay. I see your Daddy found you, eh? You know I love you Bud but I want you to be with your Daddy now and have a happy life. I'll always think of you and love you." Turning to Sean he said, "Get me out of here." He headed for the door. He was slumped over like a man twice his age.

Chapter 29

The decision for Tommy to be left in the custody of his natural father Dave Byers had been approved.

As promised, Sean held a press conference and he briefed the reporters on what he could tell them. "Tommy Byers has been found alive and well. We are still investigating the details and talking to persons of interest. We will release the details to you as soon as we have the facts defined."

"Thank you, no we can not reveal where he is at the moment and we would ask you not to pursue this avenue at the moment. We all should be happy he is safe and well. The rest will be revealed as it should, when it should. Thank you guys, it's been a long night." Sean ended the interview.

Reports filed, those who needed to be detained are being processed and preparing for a court appearance tomorrow ... all in place for now. Leanne and Sean had completed their job, for today, and could head home for much needed sleep.

"I'm on my way Sean," Leanne said. "Need some of my dad's good muffins, a big pot of tea and a long, long sleep."

"It sounds good to me Leanne. I have one stop to make first."

"Oh, really? Wouldn't be to our 'silent psychic partner', would it?" Leanne teased.

"Might be, and then again maybe not. You will have to wait and see," Sean chided back to her.

"Love makes the world go round!" Leanne sang as she opened the door.

"Just get out of here," the door slammed shut and Sean picked up the phone.

The door opened and Leanne ducked her head back in, "Love makes the world go round."

The door shut again as the private number to Joanna rang and she answered. "Hi Sean."

"Good morning Joanna. Do you have half an hour to spare right now?" Sean asked.

"Of course I do, but you have been up all night. I saw the morning news. Have you had any breakfast?" She asked with concern in her voice. "Shouldn't you get some sleep?"

"No, I have not had breakfast and I need to unwind before sleeping so I'd like to come out if you are not busy." Sean added, "Besides your gardens will help relax me."

Joanna's voice was so soft and sincere as she said, "You are more than welcome to spend the day in the gardens my friend, but let me prepare something for you and we can have a nice breakfast in the gardens where we had lunch yesterday."

The picture of them having lunch together replayed in his mind. He could feel that awesome warm, peacefulness that he felt in her presence move over him. "That would be wonderful! See you in ten minutes." Then he added, "Thank you Joanna, this means a lot to me."

Joanna could feel the sincerity of the comment Sean had made before saying good bye. "He is truly a really nice man ... a caring man." She thought to herself.

"I hope one day, I can get the opportunity to sit with him and allow his loved ones in spirit to bring through what he needs to let him open those closed areas of his heart to trust that God has another dream for him ... a plan and even when one dream fades and dies there is always a new plan ... a new dream to be born. Sean must learn to trust again to truly love again," she thought as she brought the tray of waffles in the warmer, butter maple syrup and coffee to the table already set with muffins, and fruit salad.

The doorbell rang and Joanna came to the door to greet Sean, looking like a fresh flower just picked from the garden.

Sean, however, showed some signs of the long night of hard work but surprisingly did not seem to affect his enthusiastic greeting as he joined Joanna in the gardens.

"Just what the doctor ordered, "Sean joked as he took the seat across from Joanna. "I think everyone should have a place like this to come to let go."

Like Leanne said, Joanna was their silent psychic partner and except for his team and Leanne, he would not usually discuss the case with anyone. He felt confident that it would be safe with Joanna and she actually was a silent partner working with the team so he let himself share with her what had transpired.

They ate and talked about the case. Sean filled her in step by step of how they had brought Tommy home and especially on some confirmation on things that Joanna had said that turned out to be 100% correct. About the seaman with the duffle bag and the lady who did not speak english that nursed Tommy.

"What is going to happen to Tommy now?" Joanna asked,

"Dave Byers has temporary custody and he is going after full custody. He will stay in the Navy but will have his family to support him in bring Tommy up and he will hire a full time nanny." Sean continued, "Baby Jana, Don and Marilyn's child, has be taken into the fostering care until Don can get himself on track and he will go for full custody of Janna. He is going to AA to start with and plans to ask that he be allowed to stay in Jana's life by visitation until he can prove himself. He has moved out of the home he shared with Marilyn."

"There are going to be some charges that will be dealt with in court against Marilyn and the guy who helped her put Tommy in the dumpster," Sean said.

"The seaman and his mother may also have to face charges in the beginning but I feel they will be dropped as they co-operated and the intent was to help not hinder," Sean said with hope in his heart. He prayed that Rev and his mother would not suffer any jail time or financial loss over poor choice that Rev made. In the end it was them who saved Tommy's life. He would have surely died in that dumpster.

The phone in Joanna's residence office rang. "Excuse me, Sean. Make yourself comfortable on the chaise lounge and I will be right back."

Sean stretched out on the chaise lounge, closed his eyes for a moment and could smell the fragrances of the flowers, feel a gentle breeze flowing over his body and drifted off to that lovely field of green grass where he saw in the distance two figures dancing and moving to beautiful music.

He felt himself drawn to a home behind a fenced yard. The gate was open and on the veranda of the house was a porch swing with two people swinging. Drawing closer, it was his mom and dad, together on the swing. They waved at him and he waved back. The two dancers came close again and he joined in the dance. He picked up Erin and held hands with Marlene and they danced and they laughed together. Marlene said to Sean, "I love you with all my heart and I know you loved me but you need to do one thing for me. You need to live well, my darling, and be all you can be for, in living and loving well you honour me." As she finished her request to him, he could hear her voice saying over and over, "Sean, you are loved! Sean you are loved!" as it faded so did the vision. With the fading, another voice was getting louder, "Sean. Sean?" but this time it was Joanna's voice calling him back to the every day-work-a-day world. "It is 3 p.m. and you said you needed to meet Leanne at 5."

For a moment he did not quite know where he was, and as he returned to his full awareness he said, "It's 3 p.m.? Sorry Joanne, I didn't mean to go to sleep, just rested my eyes for a moment and now it's 3 o'clock. I need to get home and get showered and changed. Check in with the team to see how everything is progressing with our case. I have to run."

"No problem at all Sean. You go and do what you need to do, my friend. You always know where to find me. And you are always welcome here, whether for a walk in the moonlight garden, a talk in the meditation garden, or a snooze on the chaise lounge." Joanna teased.

As they came to the door and Sean was about to leave, he stopped and turned to face Joanna. So close together they could feel the non verbal emotions they felt for each other rise inside of them. Their eyes met, their spirits touched.

Sean felt Joanna could see into his very secret places in his heart and his voice seemed strange, even to him, as he asked. "Do you think we might go out on a real date one night?"

"I think that may be arranged. When?" Joanna teased in her normal fun loving way.

"How about tonight at 8?" Sean answered with a question, surprising even himself at what came out of his mouth.

"You have a date! See you at 8." When Sean drove off, Joanna went back into the garden, where she saw the two spirits, who have visited her every day since she first met Sean. They smiled at Joanna and they turn and walk away ... hand-in-hand ... disappearing into the ethers.

The End...

or is it

A New Beginning?

Made in the USA
Charleston, SC
24 September 2014